A BROOKHAVEN PARANORMAL COZY MYSTERY
BOOK 7

HIGH HORSE

S.E. BIGLOW

For information contact; www.sarah-biglow.com

Edited by Alecia Goodman, Under Wraps Publishing

Cover Design by: Deranged Doctor Design

Print iSBN: 978-1-955988-64-3

Published by S.E. Biglow: February 2025

10 9 8 7 6 5 4 3 2 1

SPECIAL THANKS

I would like to thank all of the wonderful backers who supported this series on Kickstarter and made these books possible.

I need to give an extra special shout out to Heiko Koenig, GhostCat, pjs, John Idler, Sandy K., Anonymous Reader, Monica Kim, Matthew Walker, Ayl, Elizabeth W., Stephen Ballentine, Tracy 'Rayon' Fretwell, Julie McAtee, Melissa Showers, Kim, Kathy, Will 'It Work' Dansicker, Lisa Spaulding, Karin Baxter, Melissa, M. Kramer, Alexandra Corrsin, Katie, maileguy, Louisa Kannberg, Rob Steinberger, Brian, Anna McCluskey, Vannessa, Bridgette M. Findley, Mary E. Tallini, Amy Gentilini, Rosa, Stephanie Thomas, Taylor Park, Toby Rodgers, David Blethen, Amelia Pluck and Bonniejean Boettcher,

1

id-March in Brookhaven came faster than I'd expected. After the drama of Halloween, I think we were all grateful that the winter had seen very little in the way of town upheaval. There had been no mysteries to solve, no ghosts to chase or banish. Just quiet with the warmth of a nice fire and a hot cup of coffee.

"You look lost in thought," Tania noted as she joined me in the backyard of the B&B. The morning was unseasonably warm, so I sat in one of the chairs wrapped in a light shawl.

"Just thinking about how nice things have been the last few months," I answered, shifting position and pulling my knees up to my chest. My empty coffee mug perched on the arm of the chair forgotten.

My landlady smiled and sat beside me. I didn't need to be an empath to see that she was lighter since her ordeal. Being possessed had somehow helped her come to terms with being abducted by a deranged vampire trying to save his father who never thought he was good enough. I was happy to have my friend back.

"I can't say I've minded the calm," she agreed and sipped from her own mug.

"It finally feels like everything, and everyone is back to normal," I said with a sigh. "Or at least this town's version of normal."

She laughed. "With this place so full of magic, it is hard to think of anything as mundane."

Sometimes I still found it hard to believe I'd called Brookhaven my home for over a year and a half. Time had flown by and yet so much had changed. I was a proper witch now and had found people who accepted me. I'd discovered family, who I could lean on and found love where I never expected it would bloom. Brookhaven was absolutely where I was meant to put down roots and thrive.

"Oh, I wanted to tell you we have some guests

coming to stay for a couple of weeks," Tania noted after an amiable silence.

"That's grand," I said, sitting up and narrowly avoiding knocking my mug to the ground. A few blades of grass reacted to my sudden move, elongating without me intending to elicit the reaction. They wove together and buttressed the underside of the chair's arm, keeping the cup immobile.

"It'll be good to have some more faces around the dinner table," Tania said, not looking at me. "Things may get a little chaotic though."

"Don't worry about me. If things get too crazy, I'm sure I can crash at Maggie's for a few days."

I glanced over my shoulder and through the kitchen window. I could just make out the translucent outline of Sam inside, the B&B's resident ghost. While everyone else was relieved that the drama with the Hayes' ancestors had come to a close, none of us were happier than Sam. He hadn't said anything, but I knew he'd harbored some jealousy since those spirits had been able to possess living bodies and taste life one last time. All because they'd possessed magic in life, and he'd been mundane.

"Sam isn't going to be happy about company," I pointed out.

Tania gave a dismissive wave. "He can cope. We

all know he doesn't want anything to happen to this place. So, having business pick up is in everyone's best interests." After a moment she added, "But Beau might like a little peace and quiet."

"I'll ask Maggie if he can stay with her then."

"Gracias."

My phone beeped and I checked it to see the reminder that I needed to head to work. "I'll see you for dinner."

I carried my mug inside and after rinsing it, set it on the drying rack. Sam still hovered in the middle of the kitchen table, staring at the backyard.

"You doing okay, mate?" I called, plucking the car keys from their spot on the rack by the fridge.

"She told you we're having company?"

"She did. And that's a good thing."

"I know. I just, uh ... got used to it just being the four of us around here."

"Well, you're going to have to share your space. Just try not to be too obnoxious while they're around. We need customers to want to come back and bring all their friends."

He spun and floated out of the table before giving me an eye roll. "I will be on my best behavior." He held up his hands in what I assumed was a Scout salute before the gesture shifted into something much less family friendly.

"I'll see you later."

I made the short drive from the B&B up Main Street to High Time and found the employee lot unusually full for this early in the morning. I walked inside through an already bustling kitchen and into the locker area when I spotted Thomas, one of the cooks, tying up his dreadlocks.

"Did I forget about a staff meeting or something?" I asked as I stowed my bag in my locker.

"Sage has that meeting with the investor guy today. She wanted to have samples of everything available."

I stared at my co-worker for a minute in confusion. Investor? After a moment, it hit me. Sage had mentioned something about being approached by someone who wanted to expand High Time's reach beyond Brookhaven.

"Then I better make sure our best plants are ready," I said.

He smiled at me. "Sorry, still feels weird sometimes to know you can literally make them grow."

"Believe me, some days it feels just as strange to me, too."

He donned his apron and hurried off into the

kitchen, leaving me standing in the space alone. I ought to wish Sage good luck, but the office was empty when I stuck my head inside. Making my way into the growth room, I felt a sense of peace wash over me. This is where I'd been cultivating my skills, no pun intended. I'd managed to create something resembling a system with the plants. The far-left wall housed the most mature plants—arranged by strain, along with notes about what sort of edibles they worked best in. The plants that hadn't quite reached maturity were arranged on the wall abutting the front of the shop. And on the third wall were the tiny seedlings, just starting to pop out of their pots.

"Right you lot, we need to put our best foot forward today."

I pulled a stool over in front of the rows of adolescent plants. I was starting to get pretty good at coaxing plants to produce some extra leaves in a matter of hours. However, there was no way I could get seedlings to that point before Sage's new potential benefactor arrived.

"Oh, hey, Darcy." Sage's voice came from the doorway that separated the front of the shop from the growth room.

My boss wore a dark grey suit with a light blue blouse that complimented her eyes. She'd chosen black-framed glasses. Sage looked the part of a savvy businesswoman who'd filled a niche in her small town.

"Good luck today," I offered as I sunk the fingers of my left hand into the dirt of the pot in front of me. My fingers found the tender stem within and urged it to grow just a little taller.

Sage watched as the plant's leaves spread a little wider, soaking up the light from the grow lamps overhead. She smiled, although it didn't quite reach her eyes. I pulled my fingers from the dirt, brushing the remnants of soil off on the hem of my shirt.

"Something wrong?"

Sage adjusted her glasses. "I'm not sure if wrong is the right word for it. Nervous, maybe? I can't help but worry that we've been so successful because of the amazing things you've been able to do. Part of what has improved our bottom line is the quality of what we're able to produce. And that's got a lot to do with you, Darcy."

"You aren't planning to ship me off, are you?"

"God no. You're staying put if I have anything to say about it."

I picked up on her unspoken worry. "But you think this new investor may be disappointed if they can't replicate what you're doing here?"

She nodded. "I don't know why I even agreed to this meeting. I'm happy just serving our little corner of the world, you know?"

"Is it a done deal with this investor?"

"Nothing's been signed yet. That's why we're meeting today. And he wants a tour of our operation to get a better sense of what the needs of other locations might be. But he's already said he has a few locations scouted that would work well. He sounded really confident that this could take off."

"Well, if it doesn't feel right after you've done all that, you don't have to say yes."

"You're right." She straightened her suit jacket. "But I'm going to keep an open mind. I mean, this could be good for all of us."

"Let me know if I can help at all."

"Just keep those plants happy and healthy."

I gave her a salute and watched her retreat to the front of the shop. I settled into my usual routine of tending to each plant in turn. Once I was satisfied the older plants were in as good a shape as they could be, I turned my attention to the seedlings. I could feel the potential wafting from their pots from across the room. I couldn't quite explain it, but a sense of pride welled up within me as I studied each pot.

"You're going to do good things," I whispered to the still air.

Not thirty seconds later, my phone buzzed with an incoming call. Maggie's face flashed on the screen, and I quickly accepted the call.

"Hey you," I greeted.

"Hi, is now a bad time?"

"No. Just hanging with the plants while Sage gets ready to meet with an investor to talk about expanding the business."

"Do you think you'll be free for lunch?"

"For you, I think I can make that work."

The line went quiet for a moment. "As much as I'd love a romantic lunch with my girlfriend, it might be a little awkward. Vinnie came by the clinic this morning and asked if you and me could meet him at Ginny's at noon."

"Is something wrong?"

"I didn't get the sense that anything was wrong. But I could feel the nerves coming off him in waves. No empath ability needed."

Of everyone, Vinnie had been hit the hardest by the possession at Halloween. None of us had known he came from a magical family. Not until he'd admitted it after getting a taste of what he'd never had. The usually chipper deputy had been far more somber and withdrawn over the last few months.

"I will meet you both there."

"See you in a few hours; and give my best to Sage."

"Will do."

I ended the call just as I picked up the sound of voices from the front of the shop. Sage's was familiar, but the other, a tenor wasn't recogniz-able. It had to be the investor. I quickly stowed my phone and positioned myself by the seedlings.

"Come on now, perk up a bit. We've got someone to impress," I whispered as I pressed the tip of my right index finger to each tiny stalk.

"As you can see, we offer a wide variety of prod-ucts, both recreational and medicinal," Sage's voice came through the now open doorway. "And through here you'll see the growing operation."

I pivoted to find a man with a deep tan and bottle blond hair follow Sage into the space. He wore navy blue trousers and a white button-down shirt. His bright green eyes caught me off guard. They were nearly the same shade as the plants I was tending. I watched as he took in the space, undoing the top button on his collar and rolling up his sleeves in response to the sudden shift in warmth and humidity.

"The temperature is closely controlled to maximize plant growth," Sage explained as she rounded the tables and stood beside me. "Darcy tends our crops from planting through harvesting."

"You have only one person for that?" His voice carried a clear hint of disbelief that accentuated his Aussie accent.

"Darcy's got something of a green thumb." Sage gave a nervous hiccup of laughter. "Might even call her something of a miracle worker."

The man moved around the room, bending to study the notecards by the more mature plants. "Seems unusual a gardener would know what these plants ought to be used for."

"Like she said, I've got a special way with plants." I extended my hand. "Uh, I don't think I caught your name."

"Drake Gorman." He didn't shake my hand. In fact, his gaze narrowed, and he shrunk back, like he was afraid to get his hands dirty by touching me.

"Well, Sage runs a great operation here. You'd be lucky to work with her."

Drake moved to stand beside Sage, and I got the distinct feeling he was intentionally towering over her. "Well, we'll need to have more than just one person when we expand, obviously. They can't all be miracle workers. "

Before Sage or I could say anything else, he walked toward the door that led through the employee break area and into the kitchen. Dismissing me, he called, "The rest of the operation is through there I take it?"

"Yes. Please, follow me." Sage hurried to get in front of him.

She cast me an anxious glance over her shoulder before leading Drake out of the growth room. I understood her nerves now. Though I couldn't put my finger on it, but there was something I didn't trust about the man. I made a mental note to do some digging on him after my lunch with Maggie and Vinnie.

Before long, my phone read 11:57. I hurriedly clocked out, taking note that neither Sage nor Drake were on the premises, before making the short trek over to Ginny's cafe. I walked in and found Sage and Drake seated at a booth in the back, a stack of papers between them. I just hoped he didn't try to force her into anything before she had a chance to make an informed decision. I pivoted toward the other side of the café where Maggie and Vinnie were waiting for me.

"Sorry, things at work were a bit exciting this morning."

"I noticed the guy over there trying hard to wine and dine Sage," Maggie said, planting a kiss on my cheek as I sat beside her.

I turned my attention to Vinnie. He looked a little less stoic than he had the last few months. He even had a nervous energy about him, and I could feel his leg bouncing beneath the table, the movement jiggling the handcuffs on his belt.

"So, Vinnie, what did you want to talk to us about?"

Vinnie rubbed his hands together. "I know I haven't talked about my family much ... well, at all really since what happened on Halloween. But I've been in touch with my cousin. It's been a while, but I felt like it was time to try and reach out. So, uh ... I did, and he invited me to see his races this weekend. And I, uh, thought maybe it was time you two got to know me a little better."

2

Maggie and I looked at each other from our side of the booth. Okay, this wasn't what I'd been expecting when he'd invited us to lunch. Granted, an invitation to visit his family was odd. Still, he was opening up, because he felt comfortable with us. Aside from Tania and Ginny, we were the only other witches he knew in town. Technically Chief Hayes was magical, too, but the man hadn't said a word about his supernatural ability to transform into a mountain lion since it happened.

"What sort of racing does your cousin do?" Maggie leaned across the table with her elbows propped on the tabletop and her chin in her hands.

"Horse racing. My uncle runs the track. My cousin Ryan has been racing since he was sixteen."

"We'd love to come," I blurted.

Vinnie smiled, brightening his whole face. "Thank you. I can't explain how much this means to me." He pivoted in his seat and flagged down the server whose nameplate read, 'Georgia.' She had dark skin and hair the color of coffee beans twisted into tight curls all around her head. "Can we get three coffees?" He pointed to Maggie and I. "Whatever they want is on me."

Georgia blinked for a moment before approaching the table. "Uh, I don't think you're in my section."

"Ginny won't mind," Vinnie insisted.

She exhaled, pulled out her notepad and pen and looked at me. "What do you want?"

I was about to say my usual. Except Georgia had never been on shift when I'd been in and that seemed odd given how often I came in for lunch. I found myself distracted trying to puzzle how long she'd been working here and why we'd never crossed paths.

"Darcy?" Maggie's voice pulled me back from the brink of a mental rabbit hole.

"Sorry. I'll have a roast beef sandwich, extra tomato."

Georgia dutifully jotted it down and turned to Maggie. I waited patiently for the woman to take Vinnie's order before she hurried off towards the kitchen. The door swung open as she stepped through and Ginny appeared, carrying her trademark oversized mug. She made a beeline for the center seat at the counter and gave us an acknowledging look as she settled in.

"I've never seen that girl before," I said.

"Oh, she's Thomas's cousin. She's visiting for a while," Vinnie explained. "Ginny was nice enough to give her a job while she's here."

Now that he mentioned it, I remembered Thomas mentioning something about a cousin coming to stay for a while. Having so many new faces in town were throwing me off. I was beginning to understand how Ginny and Rick felt when I'd first come to town.

"So, does your cousin have magic?" I turned the conversation back to Vinnie.

"Yeah." His tone held the barest hint of disappointment. Maybe even a pang of jealousy. "I'm not quite sure what to call it. He's just always been in-tune with animals."

"Hmm ... Something of an empath?" Maggie suggested.

"Maybe. It's kind of like how Tania can always tell when I'm nervous or really excited. But with animals. There's no one who could calm the horses better than Ryan."

"Well, if he's anything like you, I'm sure we're both going to love him," Maggie said with a grin as Georgia returned with three cups and a full coffee pot.

"Your food should be out in a few minutes."

"Thanks." I reached out and took one of the cups perched precariously in her left hand and set it down. Her shoulders relaxed a fraction of an inch as she set the others down and filled them. She started to move away when she caught Ginny watching. When she turned back, I could see sweat starting to prickle at her hairline. "Did any of you want sugar or milk or anything else?"

"Black's fine with me," I said with a smile.

"We're good," Maggie confirmed.

Georgia hurried away again, leaving us to our conversation. I sipped my coffee, enjoying the strong brew. Vinnie fiddled with the handle of his mug.

"Not that I'm not excited to meet your family and get to know you better, but why now?"

I hoped the question didn't come off as judgmental. Vinnie rotated his cup again. "To be honest, I haven't been that close with my family in a long time. It's partly why I moved here, to get away from their constant disappointment that I wasn't like them." He let out a soft, bitter laugh. "Leave it to me to end up in a town full of magic. But even after I saw what you could both do, and what Ginny does ... somehow, I didn't feel like I was alone. Yes, I can't do magic like you all, but I still fit in. I have a place here. I guess I just feel it's time I showed my family that I don't need powers to exist in their world and I'm useful."

Maggie reached across the table and patted his wrist. "You absolutely fit in here. This wouldn't be Brookhaven without you."

"She's right. You were so welcoming when I first got here. Knowing you had my back is part of why I felt safe enough to stay here."

"And maybe, a small part of me wants to rub it in their faces that I do have a place now. Show them my amazing witch friends."

"No shame in flaunting what you've got," Maggie said with a laugh.

Vinnie laughed again and this time it sounded more free, less burdened by his long-carried shame of being mundane in a magical world. In short order, Georgia returned with our food, and I watched Vinnie slip her several bills—far more than what was needed to cover the bill and tip. She beamed at him, tucking the cash into her apron before she moved on to attend to another table.

Across the cafe, I watched Sage and Drake chatting in the back corner booth. The stack of papers didn't appear to have moved between them. Maybe that was a good sign, and she hadn't agreed to sign anything yet. With any luck, he'd give her a healthy amount of time to consider whatever offer he was bringing to the table.

"So, when exactly is the race?" Maggie set down her fork and reached for her napkin.

"This weekend on Saturday. There should be decent weather, and it also shouldn't be too packed."

"I'll be honest, I don't know much about horse racing. I didn't even know they happened this time of year," I admitted sheepishly.

"It's just the start of the season. And a lot of the running isn't exactly for betting. We'll get to see them do some practice runs before they do a few races for money. You're welcome to bet on any of the formal races. Don't worry I won't be offended if you don't pick Ryan's horse."

"I'm not much of a gambler," I replied.

"Me either." Maggie's posture shifted with her shoulders hunching. Her lips barely parted as she spoke. We'd never talked much about gambling, but I never got the sense it was something she was against. But her reaction to the topic seemed rather visceral.

This wasn't the time or place to push the question, so I kept my mouth shut about it. Instead, I enjoyed my sandwich and the company of my friends before my phone buzzed reminding me that I needed to get back to work.

"I'm guessing we're going to need to drive out to the track?" I downed the rest of my coffee.

"I'll give you the address. We could meet there at about ten o'clock. Everything gets underway at about eleven. So, that gives us time to check in with Ryan beforehand," Vinnie answered He pushed out of the booth and straightened his uniform shirt and holster. "I'm so glad you are both going to be able to make it."

I offered him a small wave as he strode out of the cafe. I turned in my seat, following him as he disappeared down Main Street. I stood up and moved out of the booth, so Maggie could slide out, too. Knowing that Sage would be able to tell if I got back to High

Time late—and not wanting to make her look bad in front of Drake—I planted a quick kiss on Maggie's lips.

"I guess I'll see you in the morning then."

She looped her arm through mine. "I can walk you back to work."

I glanced over my shoulder and offered Sage a small wave. She didn't see me, but I felt better for having done it. Maggie and I strolled out of Ginny's and back across Main Street toward High Time.

"That was kind of weird, right? Why isn't he offering for all of us to go together?" I blurted once we were clear of the row of shops that sat at the heart of town.

"I mean, Rick pays him decently. But I don't know that I've ever seen him driving anything except a department vehicle," Maggie replied. "Maybe he was embarrassed to ask us for a ride?"

"Maybe." I pulled my arm free and spun to block Maggie's way forward. "Have you ever met someone who could feel things from animals?"

"You seem to feel a great many things from Beau."

"That's because he's a telepath," I reminded her. "I'm serious. I've never met anyone who could do that. It's kind of like Dr. Doolittle."

"I'm impressed you know the reference," she

teased. "But I wouldn't go around making the comparison. We want these people to like us, remember? For Vinnie's sake."

I smirked. "We are both very likable. I'd dare say we're charming even."

"Well, then we are going to charm the socks off of them."

I gave her another kiss and started walking again. Too fast we had reached the employee entrance to the dispensary. She gave me a bow with a hand flourish. I couldn't help but laugh as she pivoted on her heel and went back the way we'd come. Turning to open the door, I found Sam hovering partway through the metal. He was dressed in a black sequin dinner jacket paired with a vibrant blue bowtie. His eye liner matched the tie, and he'd somehow managed to add tiny rhinestones to his left cheek.

"Bloody hell, don't do that!" I gasped.

"There's a stranger in town," he announced.

I made a shooing gesture, and he vanished into the door. I hurried through the kitchen and break room back into the grow room, shutting the door behind me. Sam rematerialized between a row of seedlings.

"You've seen him, right? Tall, kind of handsome. Accent."

"His name is Drake Gorman. He's here trying to convince Sage to expand High Time."

"Shady for sure," he declared.

"Or he's just looking to enter into a business agreement with her. For all we know he's got the marketing know-how to bring High Time to the next level. Sage deserves every success she can have. And anything I can do to make that happen, I will."

"So, you're going to clone yourself?" he teased.

"If I have to ... or work extra hours."

"Magical burnout is no joke, Darcy. You need to be careful that's the sort of thing you don't ever come back from."

"Thanks for the tip. But really, you don't need to worry. Sage knows what she's doing."

"I still don't trust the guy. Maybe it's the accent."

"I've got an accent, thank you."

"Yeah, but yours is all sweet and cheery. His is ... scary."

"You'd be singing a different tune if he could see you," I teased.

"I stand by what I said." He fiddled with his bowtie, but didn't meet my gaze. "Oh, what did Deputy Ditzy want?"

"You've got to stop calling him that. Vinnie is my friend. And while he might not be able to see you anymore, he knows you exist. I won't have you making fun of people I care about."

"Relax, Darcy. It's just a pet name. I'm fond of the guy. So, what did he want?"

"He's invited Maggie and I to meet some of his family this weekend. His cousin is like a horse whisperer or something, and races. It's a big deal for him to even ask us."

"Actually, it's a big deal for him to even mention he's got family," Sam muttered. "I don't know much about horses. I'm not really an animal person. Or I wasn't when I was alive anyway."

"You seem to get on well enough with Beau."

"He's a category all his own," Sam said with a mischievous sparkle in his eye. "Well, do try to stay out of trouble while you're gone. I know that's like asking water not to be wet. But still, I know Tania would scold me if I didn't try and remind you."

"I have no intention of getting into any sort of trouble. What could possibly go wrong? It's just horses racing around a track, isn't it?"

"Oh, honey, when betting is involved, anything and everything can go wrong. You could lose everything, or you could become richer than the Queen."

He tapped his chin. "Well, maybe not that last part. More like small town rich."

"That's assuming I gamble at all, which I don't intend to."

"I'm just telling you, if something can go wrong, it will. And when it does, you stay the hell out of it. We don't need you getting mixed up in some weird animal shenanigans."

"You have my word, I will not get involved in any shenanigans."

He leaned in close and tapped my chin. Or he would have if he were corporeal. "Don't make promises you can't keep."

"Look, I just want to have a nice time with my friends. Is that too much to ask?"

"Around here? Yes."

I heard the sounds of voices echoing from the front of the dispensary. It sounded like Sage had come back and Drake was with her. There was every possibility they could walk in and see me talking to myself. Well, that wouldn't help Sage's business at all.

"Right, you need to get out of here. I've got to get back to work."

Sam gave an exaggerated sigh and did a twirl mid-air, his feet a good six inches off the ground.

"Fine. But I'm telling you, even if you don't go looking for trouble, it's bound to find you. That's just how this always works, Darcy."

I wanted to tell him that he was wrong, and I was capable of having a nice day out at the races. Though, as I looked back at my time here in town, I knew he was right. No matter what I tried to do that was supposed to be 'normal,' it always ended up mired in some magical mystery or problem. Maybe this time would be the exception. I could only hope.

3

———

$\mathcal{S}$aturday morning came bright and early. I woke to my alarm beeping at me from the side table at a little after seven thirty. I let out a soft groan, intending to roll over when I felt something small and spiky hit my forearm. I opened one eye to find Beau curled up on my other pillow, blinking at me.

'Can't sleep in.'

"Oh, come on, just a few more minutes," I pleaded.

He cocked his head to one side, blinked at me as if to communicate his disapproval before he scurried across my torso and hopped down off the bed. Not wanting him to send in reinforcements, I dragged myself out of bed and made my way to the bathroom. A quick shower was enough to wake me up properly and as the clock struck eight, I stood back in my bedroom staring at my closet. I wore my robe over an oversized t-shirt Maggie had lent me months ago as I tried to pick the right outfit for the occasion.

A soft knock on the door drew my attention and Tania poked her head in. "It's a big day."

"It's just a trip to a racetrack with friends," I corrected.

Tania gestured, asking without words if she could enter. I waved her in, and she eased the door open far enough to cross the threshold. "You are getting to see a part of Vinnie's life he doesn't share with many people. That is a big deal."

"Is that a note of jealousy I just heard?" I teased.

"I have always had a sense that he was very private, even without my magical gifts. I've respected his desire for privacy. But I am curious to see the kind of people he comes from."

"In a way, it's my situation just in reverse," I said as I pushed aside my short-sleeved shirts for the long-sleeved blouses. It might be March, but it was still chilly. "Though, I'm pretty sure I wouldn't want him meeting my parents."

"Just try to remember that families of all kinds are complicated. But look at it this way, you'll have something in common with them. Lean into that. It can't hurt to have some more magical people in your circle."

I wasn't sure I wanted to expand my magical circle given the drama we'd just endured a few months ago, but I kept quiet. This was the most animated I'd seen Tania in a while, and I didn't want to spoil her mood.

"I promise I'll keep an open mind."

"Good."

"Could you help me figure out what I'm supposed to wear? I want to make a good impression."

Tania gave me a smile as she stepped up beside me, surveying the clothing hanging in the closet. She tapped her chin in thought for a while before reaching in and pulling out a simple dark blue top. "This one, I think."

She quickly grabbed a pair of jeans, and I found some ankle-high boots in the back of the closet that completed the look. She left me to change. I found her downstairs over a griddle, flipping pancakes. Thick strips of bacon sizzled in a pan to her left and I could smell fresh squeezed orange juice from across the kitchen.

"I know this is a big deal for Vinnie, but why do I

get the feeling you're in hostess mode?" I took the plate of pancakes she offered me to the table. I plucked a few off the serving tray, burning my finger-tips as I did so, and hastily tossed them onto another plate.

"Well, I'm sure you know that Sage has been in talks with someone about investing in the dispensary."

"Yeah. I met him yesterday when she was giving him a tour of the place. I know she's nervous about the whole thing."

"Well, I could sense her anxiety a mile off and I figured it might be nice to bring her something. So, I've been up since first light trying to decide on that something."

"That's really nice of you. I'm sure she'll appreciate it. And your company."

She carried the bacon over and joined me at the table. "I think I'll appreciate her company, too." She didn't meet my gaze as she spoke. "You, Maggie, and Ginny have been so supportive these last months. And I am so grateful, but while you are eager to dive deeper into your magic, as you should be, I need a bit of a step back."

"And since I came out to everyone, Sage knows

about the existence of magic. But she's not going to ask you about it."

"No. She is not."

"Well, I'm sure you're going to have a great time, whatever you decide to bring her." I glanced around the space, taking in the absence of our usual chatty ghost. "Where's Sam?"

"I think he got a little pouty that I was baking, and he couldn't have anything. Since the whole possession, he's been rather touchy about being incorporeal."

"He came by the dispensary today. He seemed awfully concerned about Sage's meeting with the investor."

"He doesn't like change."

"It's not like he'd be going anywhere. Or that Sage and the dispensary would uproot or anything."

"Right, but it means more new people poking around town. And he is something of a creature of habit after all his years of afterlife."

"I can't say I've met many ghosts obviously, but none have been such a diva," I admitted.

Tania laughed. "Don't let you hear him say that. It might go to his head."

I couldn't help but laugh a little, too. We fell into

companionable silence over our pancakes and fresh juice. Half an hour later, I stood over the sink, washing dishes. My phone sat on the counter well out of the splash zone of the sink and began skittering as it vibrated with an incoming call from Maggie.

Tania reached over and tapped the little green accept button and set it to speaker for me. "Morning, beautiful," my girlfriend greeted.

"Careful, you're on speaker," I warned her.

"Buenas dias, Maggie," Tania called.

"Hi, Tania. Okay Darcy, I was just calling, because Vinnie texted me the address. It looks like it's a couple of hours away. So, I was going to come by now and pick you up."

"Yesterday he made it seem like it was close by."

"Maybe it's drawing a bigger crowd than he had thought, but my app says there's a lot of traffic. And we don't want to be late."

"No, of course. I'll be ready."

"See you soon."

The call ended and I stood there looking at my phone for a moment. I couldn't quite put into words what I was feeling. Sure, I was excited to meet Vinnie's family, and a little nervous, too. But I thought I'd had more time to get those emotions in check.

Tania patted my shoulder. "You're going to be fine. Just be yourself. They'll love you two."

The way she looked at me told me she'd sensed my apprehension. "Thanks."

She made a shooing gesture and took over my spot at the sink. I hastily dried my hands and pulled on my coat just as my phone buzzed with a text from Maggie letting me know she was waiting outside. I hurried out to meet her, sliding into the passenger seat of her car.

"Ready to find out everything you never knew you wanted to know about our lovable deputy?" Maggie asked as she put the car in reverse.

"I hope so."

Maggie settled her phone in the stand on her dashboard and I watched as the map app routed us out of Brookhaven and up north. True to her word, it said it would take us nearly two hours to reach our destination. As we passed the station, I realized we ought to let Vinnie know about the traffic.

"Did you let him know we were heading out?"

"Yeah, I sent him a note right before I called you. Haven't heard back though. But I'm sure it will be fine."

"Then I guess we'll just see him there."

I rested my head against the headrest and looked

out the window at the passing scenery. It really was beautiful here, even with many of the trees not yet fully recovered from the winter weather. It felt peaceful. The phone periodically gave Maggie directions. Since I wasn't the one driving, I didn't pay them much mind.

When I looked at the car clock, it read 9:17. Maggie shifted in her seat, her dark brown jacket's zipper rubbing against the seat. She looked uncomfortable and I could see by the way her hands gripped the steering wheel that she was carrying tension in her shoulders.

"Something's bothering you."

She glanced at me for a moment before focusing on the road. "I'm fine."

"You're tense. That's not like you. What's going on?"

She didn't answer. The tiny dot on the map continued to move along a blue path, fast approaching a long stretch of red that signaled we were about to hit that traffic she'd mentioned earlier. Sure enough a few minutes later, she eased the car to a halt. Taillights glinted in the early morning light as far as the eye could see.

"We're going to be stuck here a while, you might

as well talk to me, Maggie. Please. Maybe I can help?"

She let go of the steering wheel and raked her fingers through her short red mop of hair. "It's the gambling."

"I got the sense yesterday you're not a fan. I don't think Vinnie's expecting us to place bets. We're going there to meet his family."

"Just being around gambling, it makes me uncomfortable."

Am I about to find out my girlfriend has a secret gambling addiction?

"I'm going to need more than that."

She let out a long, audible exhale. "A long time ago, I got into some online gambling. It wasn't that serious, but my brother found my accounts. I stepped away from it all, because I didn't like what it was doing to me. He wasn't so lucky."

"You never told me any of this."

"I like to keep some things private, Darcy."

"And you're afraid it might ... trigger a relapse?"

"Not exactly. Like I said, it wasn't that serious for me. But him ... let's just say it got to a point where we stopped speaking because all he ever wanted was money to settle up with his bookies."

"Did he get into horses?"

"A little bit, yeah. I know most of it was online, but for all I know it could have progressed to live events, too. It's just part of my life I'd rather forget."

"You could have told Vinnie you weren't comfortable coming."

"I've known Vinnie for a while, and he's never opened up like this with anyone before. I want to be a supportive friend. I didn't want to let my personal drama dampen his mood or overshadow what he was trying to do."

I reached over and grabbed her right hand in my left. "Well, whatever I can do to make this easier for you, just tell me and I'll do it."

"You being with me helps. Really. And ... maybe not mentioning it to Vinnie?"

"My lips are sealed."

"Thank you."

The brake lights ahead of us eased up and the cars started inching forward. Soon, we were on our way again, moving at a respectable speed. The estimated time of arrival on her phone said we'd get there right at ten o'clock. Still, there was no responding message from Vinnie or indication that he'd even seen Maggie's text. It worried me. Part of me feared he'd regretted his decision and would back out, leaving us two hours from home with strangers in a place that made my girlfriend exceedingly nervous.

"Maybe I should call him, just to check in?" I offered.

"Good idea."

I pulled up the newly created contact for Vinnie in my phone and hit 'Call.' The line rang five times before going to voicemail. "Uh hey, Vinnie, it's Darcy. Just letting you know that we're on the way, but we hit some traffic. Maggie sent you a message about the traffic earlier. Hopefully, you're not stuck in it, too. Anyway, we'll see you soon."

I hung up and stowed my phone in my jacket pocket. There wasn't much else we could do besides keep moving forward. Whatever had caused the jam smoothed out and before we knew it, we were turning off the highway onto a series of winding roads that led to a tall complex with stadium seating. I could see the rows of seats rising up in the distance, getting more defined as we approached.

Our assumption that the races were attracting more than normal spectators proved accurate as we pulled into the parking lot. Almost every spot was filled. We managed to squeeze into a spot at the very end. I was about to step out of the car when I heard the roar of an engine approaching and a motorcycle zipped by. I'd have clipped the driver with the door if I'd gotten out. The biker turned back and pulled into one of the remaining spots in the next row over.

"What a jerk!" I said as I climbed out of the car.

"Just leave it. We need to go find Vinnie," Maggie called.

Logically, I knew she was right, and yet I couldn't stop my feet from moving forward. I approached the figure still sitting astride the motorcycle. "I could have hit you," I called, pointing back at Maggie's car.

I expected the driver to tell me off. Instead, they pulled their helmet off to reveal Vinnie. "Sorry, Darcy. I didn't mean to get that close."

"Vinnie? Since when do you drive a motorcycle?" I blurted. I pivoted to look at Maggie. "Did you know about this?"

"Never seen it before in my life."

Vinnie's cheeks flushed in embarrassment. "I've had my license for a few years. I bought this when I made deputy. I know it's not a huge salary bump, but it felt like something I should celebrate. Usually, it just sits under a cover behind my apartment. I figured today was a good day to break it out."

I couldn't help myself and burst out laughing. "You want to show your cousin how cool and tough you are. Mr. Lawman with your fancy motorcycle and sexy leather jacket."

He brushed off the jacket. "You think it's sexy?"

"Come on. Let's go meet your family before you both draw more attention," Maggie suggested, ushering us towards the entrance. It was only then that I realized several of the other attendees were watching us very closely.

I looped my arm through Maggie's and held her close. I couldn't explain why, but their leering looks made me suspicious. Sam's warning about not getting into shenanigans echoed in my head as we approached the gate. From his mouth to the universe's proverbial ear.

4

———————

As we joined the line of attendees waiting to get in, I really took a look at Vinnie. He'd dressed in tight jeans and thick soled boots. He wore a solid black shirt beneath his leather jacket, with a smattering of silver zippers on the front and sleeves. This was not the man I'd come to associate with the gentle lawman in Brookhaven. He looked like someone I'd run into on the Tube in London and try to avoid. Vinnie looked rough and dare I say badass. He'd even slicked his hair back from his face.

"So, when's the last time you saw your cousin Ryan?" I asked, stepping up beside him as the queue moved forward.

"About ten years ago," he admitted.

"That's a long time not to talk to someone." Then again, I suspected it could take that long before I spoke to my parents again.

"We were closer as kids. I knew he went into the family business. I lost touch with so many relatives, and we just kind of drifted apart."

"Does he know what you do for a living?" Maggie piped up.

"I mean, he knows I went to school for criminal justice. But ... no, he doesn't know about my job."

"Well, that explains the get up," I said with a smile. "I'm guessing you were something of a wild child?"

"I had a certain swagger," he agreed. "But then I got serious and that part of me took a backseat. And I was okay with that."

"So, you don't know how much he's changed in that time either. And you want him to be able to recognize you," Maggie pointed out.

"Something like that."

"You said what happened at Halloween prompted you to reach out. How'd he feel about that?" I stepped forward in the line.

"He was a little surprised. But he told me he'd been thinking about trying to reach out to me, too. So, I guess it was just time. He'd always been around horses when we were younger, but he hadn't started racing when we drifted apart. I was kind of surprised when he told me he'd finally got into jockeying."

"Did he say where we should meet him?" I probed.

"He said he'd leave us some special passes. Once we make it through the ticketing, we should be able to head to the stables. "

We were about to find out if Ryan was true to his word. We had reached the front of the queue. Vinnie gave his details and the ticket taker handed over three tickets along with three lanyards and plastic badges reading 'Special Access.'

I slid the lanyard over my head and took the ticket he offered me. Maggie did the same and we tapped the tickets at the turnstile. I spotted a man with dark brown hair pacing on the other side. He sported the same complexion as Vinnie, and I could see similarities in their facial features. But where Vinnie was tall and lanky, Ryan was shorter and even thinner. He wore riding boots and pants, with an oversized jacket that poorly hid the jockey uniform underneath.

"Look at you!" Vinnie called, catching the man's attention. "You haven't changed a bit."

Ryan looked up and his shoulders relaxed. He

crossed the distance and pulled Vinnie into a hug, clapping him firmly on the back. "I was starting to think you weren't going to show, Cuz."

"Traffic was a bear getting here," Vinnie answered. "I've never seen this place so packed at the start of the season."

"New ownership. They've been doing a lot of marketing to get people to come in early." He didn't sound enthused by that change. "Come on, let's head to the stables. I think there's someone who'll be happy to see you."

Maggie and I fell into step behind Vinnie and Ryan, letting them guide us away from the ticket windows. People were already starting to place bets and study racing brackets. I gave Maggie's hand a firm squeeze as she scanned the faces. She relaxed a touch when we were away from the area, and I assumed she hadn't seen her brother. We followed Ryan and Vinnie down a long corridor that dead ended in a metal door. Ryan tapped a keycard to the locking mechanism, and with a loud beep it opened. For a moment, that seemed like excessive security until I realized just how much money was likely invested in the horses racing today. Horse racing was a rather lucrative business.

The door led to another corridor that fed into a

large barnlike structure. Jockeys and other personnel moved around the space, some leading horses into and out of stalls. We moved all the way to the end of the space where a sleek grey horse stood in a stall. It chomped at the bit in its mouth. The beast's gaze darted around, tracking the flurry of activity.

"Hey there, look who came to see you," Ryan said in a soft tone as he approached the horse. The creature let out a chuffing sound and took a step back as Ryan reached out a hand. "Easy now, girl. Easy."

"Hey Lightspeed, you remember me?" Vinnie's voice dropped to a low tone, and he held out a hand for the horse to sniff. It's nostrils flared at his attempt to make contact, but she didn't back up further. "I know it's been a while."

"She's been antsy all morning," Ryan explained.

"Maybe she knew Vinnie was coming?" I suggested.

"I may have let it slip," Ryan admitted.

"I was there when Lightspeed was born," Vinnie explained. "I helped break her in as a foal, too. I didn't think she was still racing."

Ryan let out a long breath. "I told Dad we needed to retire her. But she's one of our fastest still. He thinks she's got a few more races in her. He's hoping the rest of the season."

"You don't sound convinced." Maggie took a step closer to the stall.

"Like Vin said, she's getting up there in age. She deserves to have a nice retirement."

"You're riding her?" Vinnie pointed to the jockey uniform Ryan sported.

"That was the only way I'd agree to let Dad keep racing her. I don't trust anyone else with her."

Vinnie glanced at Maggie and me. "You can tell them why. They'll understand."

"We know you, uh ... commune with animals," I said, hoping I hadn't just completely offended him. "Sort of like an empath, right?"

"Yeah, something like that. How exactly do you know about that?"

"My landlady's an empath. And I'm a hedge witch," I answered. I spotted some hay piled on the ground up against the far wall. I concentrated and the strands began to weave together, climbing up towards the ceiling.

"And I'm a healer," Maggie added.

The hay continued to wind together, taking on the shape of a horse's head that looked remarkably like the gray mare in front of us. Out of nowhere, the horse began to whinny and kick up her front feet. I let the hay drop back into the pile it had come from.

"I didn't mean to frighten her," I said.

Ryan didn't respond. He was too busy trying to get her to settle down. He reached for the reins hanging from her bridle as she continued to rear up and kick at the stall door. Vinnie grabbed Maggie and I by the hand leading us away, to give Ryan space to work. I watched as his cousin whispered to the mare with his hands pressed firmly to her flank as he did so. I turned to look at the rest of the stable to see if any of the other horses were similarly spooked. They all looked unaffected by my magical display. In fact, none of the jockeys appeared to even notice what was going on at our end of the space. Though I did sense someone watching us. Except when I turned around, no one was there.

"I'm so sorry, didn't mean to scare her," I said, as Ryan finally managed to get her settled back down. "I just wanted to show you that you are among friends, that's all."

Ryan's cheeks were flushed as he patted Lightspeed on the nose and rested his forehead against the side of her stall. "It's not you. She's been skittish lately. I keep telling her there's nothing to worry about, but you can't exactly reason with a horse. No matter how much I might want to."

"We should let you get ready for the race. We don't want to interrupt any pre-race rituals the two of you have," Maggie said, tugging my arm so that I had no choice but to back up a few paces.

"I got you seats in the VIP box. Your passes should get you up there. I'll see you after the races. We're only in the first two this morning."

"Good luck!" I called as Vinnie led us back out of the stables and to the spectator area. As we wound our way through the stands to the large, enclosed space marked VIP, I spotted several security guards surveying the perimeter. They were armed with radios and guns.

"The artillery looks a bit overkill, even for a race-track," I said to Vinnie, gesturing to one of the guards passing by.

His brow furrowed as he studied the man in the grey security uniform. "Obviously, they don't want people making off with the money."

"Wouldn't things like batons and stun guns work just as well? I'd have to imagine having loaded weapons around horses isn't a good idea," I protested.

"I guess a lot has changed since I was around the

place last," Vinnie answered and settled into one of the front row seats.

"Are we going to get to meet your uncle while we're here?" I settled in beside him. "I'm assuming that's who Ryan meant when he said his dad?"

"You might. When he comes by to watch any of his horses race, he's usually up here."

"I get the feeling you don't particularly get along with him," Maggie said from his other side.

"Ryan was understanding when we were kids, that I was different from the rest of the family. His dad wasn't exactly the nicest guy to anyone. He was motivated by success and prestige. I'm guessing that's why he's made Ryan keep racing Lightspeed even though she's past her prime."

"How did he feel about Ryan's gift?" Maggie tugged her jacket off and laid it over the back of her chair. I did the same.

"From what I remember, at least when we were kids, he thought it made Ryan weak. Almost like he wasn't as much of a man, because he had this more sensitive, softer side. I guess he's realized how it benefits him with the horses to let Ryan use his gifts that way."

"What's his gift, then?" I asked.

"He could see the future. Nothing huge, just enough he knew what bets to place to make money."

"Guess he's in the right business, then," Maggie noted.

"He was always flaunting it around us, too. Like it made him better than everyone else," Vinnie muttered.

"Family is so bloody complicated," I sighed.

"You're telling me."

The door to the VIP booth opened a couple of times and one of the security officers poked his head inside. Vinnie showed him our Special Access passes and he disappeared again. The next time the door opened, a burly man with greying temples and an intense gaze walked in. Vinnie sat up a little straighter.

"I heard you might be here," the man stated, looking at Vinnie with an air of disappointment that his sacred space had been violated.

"Ryan invited us. Maggie, Darcy this is my Uncle Reese."

I stood up and offered my hand. I stared him straight in the face, giving him no other choice but to shake my hand. He gripped it in a vice like gesture. "And what do you do?"

"I help sell magically infused weed," I said.

"Maggie is a healer. And we are grateful to have Vinnie keeping the peace in our town."

Reese's brows arched. "Keeping the peace, huh?"

"He's the deputy in Brookhaven. Second in command to the Chief of Police," Maggie added. "We owe a lot to him."

"Thought I heard you went straight." Coming from Reese, it sounded like an insult.

I could see the color rise in Vinnie's cheeks, but he stayed seated. "I'm not here in any official capacity. I'm just looking to support my cousin in doing something he loves. That's all."

Reese let out a grumble, but took a seat in the back of the VIP box. I turned my attention to the track down below. I could see fans filling the stands as the time ticked closer to the start of the race. A few of the jockeys and their horses were over in a grassy area, jumping hurdles and preparing for their own races. I didn't see Lightspeed among them.

After maybe ten minutes, the jockeys and horses disappeared. A hush fell over the stands as I leaned forward in my seat, watching the row of gates down and off to the left. I could see a few horse heads poking out from behind the starting gates. I stared hard until I found Lightspeed at the innermost spot.

"Let's go Ryan!" I shouted as the starting gun

went off, even though he couldn't hear me from all the way up here.

The gates went down, and the horses took off. I tracked the movement from the inner lane as Lightspeed took a stumbling start out of the gate. She certainly wasn't living up to her name. Even from this distance I could tell something wasn't right. She couldn't keep her legs under her when she ran and she stopped, her flank heaved heavily. Ryan did his best to urge her onward, but it was as if she was completely unaware of his presence. I didn't know much about horses, but I knew this wasn't a good sign. I hadn't noticed her balance was off earlier when we'd been in the stable. Had my little magic display done more damage than I'd originally thought?

I looked to Vinnie for some clue as to what might be going on, but his gaze was glued to the scene unfolding down on the track. I turned to watch Reese's reaction. He remained settled back in his seat, apparently unconcerned about his horse or his son. Down on the track, other jockeys whose horses were already coming around for another pass slowed to take in the spectacle. Even the announcers had gone quiet, clearly unsure of what to make of the horse's behavior. Slowly, Lightspeed took another shaky step forward before her legs gave out completely. She crumpled to the ground, rolling onto her side.

Ryan slid off the saddle onto the track. I gripped the edges of my seat as I tracked his movements. Somehow, he got to his feet. He looked disoriented as he swayed and took a step before he, too, collapsed.

5

The entire stadium froze in horror at the sight of Lightspeed and Ryan laying on the track. I could already feel the knot of dread tightening in my gut as the suspicion that something was seriously amiss hit me. I couldn't help but look at Vinnie to gauge his reaction. He was already out of his seat and barreling towards the VIP box door. I was on my feet a few seconds later, trailing him down to the ground level. I glanced back once over my shoulder to see Maggie bringing up the rear. His Uncle Reese hadn't moved from his spot in the VIP box.

That seemed strange, given that his own son had just collapsed and from what I'd witnessed didn't appear to be moving. The other racers had stopped, much to the crowds dismay and two of the jockeys who'd been closest to the incident dismounted. Their horses pawed the ground and let out loud neighs as their riders left them unattended. A pang hit me that Ryan could have calmed them down if he'd been conscious.

"Please be all right," I whispered as Vinnie burst through the partition separating spectators from the track itself.

"You can't go out there," one of the security guards shouted, hand on the holster at his hip.

I moved to block the man's path. "That's his cousin. He's just trying to make sure he's okay. Let him through. Please."

The guard's gaze darted from the scene on the track back to me and he eased up. "The rest of you stay back."

In that moment, I wished Sam were here. He might have been invisible to most of the people in the audience, but he could have told me what was happening. Even Beau could have given me a blow-by-blow. Except neither of my supernatural mates had come along for this one. Maggie, while magical, was stuck behind the scenes with me.

"I'm a medic!" Maggie yelled at the guard as Vinnie fell to his knees beside Ryan. One of the other jockeys was leaning over Ryan, hands pressed against his sternum administering CPR.

Her words didn't sway the guard keeping us at bay. So, all we could do was watch as Vinnie pulled out his phone and dialed 9-1-1. I could hear his words filtering through the air as a hush settled over the crowd. The announcers had fallen silent, too.

"I have a twenty-nine-year-old male unresponsive after a fall from a horse. He's unconscious and barely breathing. Send an ambulance. Now!"

I admired the way Vinnie could stay so calm with his family member—estranged or not—in such peril. One of the other jockeys had gone to stand beside the fallen horse. The security guard who'd been keeping us at bay turned his attention to a few other onlookers trying to take some cellphone shots and I hurried along the barrier to get closer to Lightspeed.

"What happened?" I called, pointing to the downed mare.

"She's dead," he answered. He knelt beside her and stroked her neck.

I couldn't shake the feeling something was off about the whole thing. Yes, she'd been spooked earlier, but that shouldn't have accounted for her strange behavior at the start of the race. And while she'd collapsed onto her side, the mare hadn't landed on Ryan. There was no logical reason for him to have collapsed, too.

Trouble follows you.

Sam had warned me. Surely, I wasn't the reason any of this was happening. But I was here and if something had gone wrong with Ryan, I had no doubt Vinnie would be the first to try and track down the truth. Even if it was on an unofficial basis since he had no authority out here. We were far beyond Brookhaven's jurisdiction.

I turned back to the VIP box. Reese was still sitting there. Maybe his view had been obstructed before or he didn't realize it was Ryan who'd fallen? But no, it was obvious now who was injured. I looked at Maggie. "This feels off."

"Glad I'm not the only one who thinks so."

"But I don't know what to do or say."

"We wait for help to get here and then we ask Vinnie how he wants us to support him."

I noticed she didn't say a word about wanting to go looking around. Yet, I could see the way that she kept looking back and to the right, towards the stables. She was itching to go snooping. We made quite the pair.

In the distance, sirens wailed, growing louder as

the emergency personnel arrived on scene. I stepped closer to Maggie as the doors that led in from the turnstiles opened and two medics carrying a stretcher rushed onto the track. Vinnie and the other jockey stepped back, allowing the medics to continue lifesaving measures. As Vinnie stepped back, I could see his hands shaking. He'd seen unimaginable things on his job. I'd witnessed many of them myself, but I'd never seen a family member in such a state.

"Ladies and gentlemen, the rest of the morning's races are suspended until further notice. We apologize for the inconvenience. Anyone who wishes to receive a voucher for a return ticket should proceed to the ticketing gates," one of the announcers called over the intercom.

The space filled with the sounds of hundreds of footsteps moving through the stands and back towards the exits. I watched them go and something else felt not right. What was it? "Wait! They can't leave," I blurted to no one in particular.

"What are you talking about?" a woman seated in the row directly behind me said.

"A man's just collapsed under strange circumstances. We're all witnesses. The police will need to question us."

She let out a haughty laugh. "You're crazy if you think people are going to stick around for that sort of thing."

But they didn't have a choice. The police needed to conduct an investigation. I had no doubt Vinnie would insist on it. In fact, with security busy keeping the emptying stands orderly, no one was there to keep me from getting onto the track. I moved to stand beside Vinnie.

"This doesn't feel right," I said.

"Ryan was fine before the race. He shouldn't have collapsed."

"I know. I'm sorry."

The medics loaded Ryan onto the stretcher and positioned an oxygen mask over his nose and mouth. One of the medics positioned himself over Ryan's torso on top of the stretcher, continuing compressions. "Go!"

The stretcher disappeared back the way the medics had come and soon the other jockeys began to lead their horses in the direction of the stables. No one had come to attend to Lightspeed. I left Vinnie's side and bent down beside the horse. Her eyes were still open, but they were unseeing; lifeless. I tried to close the one that looked up at me. Though her body didn't cooperate with me.

I was no veterinarian, but I couldn't see any obvious signs that would have caused the horse's balance issues or her fall. I ran my hands along the side of her neck and along her flank beneath the saddle. Nothing felt out of place. But something had clearly caused the mare severe issues.

"What happened to you?" In that moment, I wished I had Ryan's ability to commune with animals. If her spirit lingered at all, maybe I could have found a clue.

As I moved to stand up, I caught something sticking out of the corner of her mouth. It looked like a piece of hay. But why would Ryan feed her right before a race? That didn't seem like the right thing to do. Besides, if she was a racehorse, she'd surely have a strict diet including special feed. As gently as I could, I peeled her lips apart and plucked the strand of hay from between her teeth.

My head began to swim as I held it. Hay wasn't exactly alive, but my powers had been expanding for a while. I'd been able to revive nearly dead grasses in the past. It stood to reason if there was something this particular piece of hay could tell me, my magic was clinging to it.

Come on, show me what you know.

My heart thumped against my ribs as the world

continued to fade in and out of equilibrium. I tried to stand up, but my balance was off kilter. I took a step back and it was as if my entire lower extremities had gone numb. I stumbled away from the horse, my vision tunneling to grey.

Suddenly I felt a pair of strong hands wrap around my biceps and hold me steady. "Darcy, what's going on?"

I could hear the concern in Vinnie's tone. I blinked and slowly, my vision cleared. He stood in front of me, staring at me as if I'd grown a second head. I swallowed the cottony feeling from my mouth and held out the piece of hay. "Vinnie, I think whatever happened might have been foul play."

"What makes you think that?" His voice was low, conspiratorial.

"I found this in Lightspeed's mouth and when I touched it, , I felt really ill. Like part of my body was numb. I couldn't control my balance and my vision went wonky. Using my magic made it worse."

"Like what happened with Lightspeed at the start of the race?" he said.

"I think we ought to go have a look around the stable and see if someone might have put something in her hay to throw the race."

"And not to sound judgmental, but your uncle

hasn't moved from the VIP box. Even after seeing Ryan carried out on a stretcher," Maggie added, joining us on the track.

"They've always had a strained relationship, but even I know Reese wouldn't just sit by while his son suffered."

"So, what do you want us to do?"

"We wait until the police come. We give our statements, and then we figure out what happened."

"Your badge doesn't mean much out here," I reminded him.

"Don't tell Rick. But sometimes, you have to go outside the normal bounds of the law to find the truth and get justice," Vinnie admitted.

"I'm sorry all of this is happening just when you were trying to reconnect with your family," I said, fixing Vinnie with a sympathetic look.

"Part of me had this fear that coming back would blow up in our faces. I'm not magical, but I've seen enough of it in my life to know that it can get in the way ... of a lot of things. I guess I'd just hoped having you two with me would have somehow mitigated it."

"It has. We have plenty of power between the two of us," Maggie replied. "Besides, it seems Darcy's already figured out where we ought to start our search."

Half the crowd had emptied out by the time a handful of uniformed police officers walked in. They didn't look particularly concerned by the scene unfolding in front of them. Vinnie wiped the sweat from his palms before approaching the man whose name patch read, 'Sgt. Higgs.'

"You the one who called 9-1-1?" Higgs asked.

"Yes, Sir. The victim is my cousin. And I should inform you that I'm a police officer myself. Out of Brookhaven."

Higgs eyed Vinnie dubiously. "You're not on duty in my jurisdiction, son."

"I understand. You should also know that that a decent number of people have left the scene, which is going to make taking witness statements more difficult."

"You let me worry about that." Higgs motioned for one of his fellow officers to join them. "He'll take your statement. Then you can go, Officer."

"It's Deputy actually," Vinnie replied.

Higgs gave a dismissive snort before walking off in the direction of the VIP box. That seemed a strange place to head when the scene was on the track ahead of him. The other officer who'd been summoned pulled out a notebook similar to one I'd seen Vinnie use dozens of times.

"How about you tell me what you saw then?"

Vinnie rubbed his chin. "We were seated up in the VIP box." He gestured overhead. "The first race started and Lightspeed, that's Ryan's horse, came out staggering. Something was clearly wrong with her. She didn't make it very far before she collapsed. Ryan didn't look like he was pinned or anything. But after he stood up, he just crumpled like he was a puppet whose strings had just been cut."

"Pretty fancy talk for a cop," the officer muttered. He looked at Maggie and me. "That what you two see as well?"

"Yes, Officer. We'd seen Ryan shortly before the race. He and Lightspeed looked fine," Maggie replied.

"Well, something had spooked her, but she appeared to be fine otherwise," I corrected. "We didn't notice anything off with her balance or anything."

"This the first time you've been to the races here?"

"Yes. We were meeting Ryan for the first time, too," I answered.

"Right. Well, we'll take a look around once we've had a chat with a few more people. You're free to go.

But I should probably take your numbers in case we have more questions."

Vinnie pulled a business card from his pocket and handed it over. "My cell phone number is on the back."

The officer pocketed the card before moving on to find other people to interview. Sgt. Higgs was still up in the VIP box talking to Reese. I couldn't gauge Reese's expression from this distance. Maybe he was just someone who was stoic in the face of adversity. Vinnie took a steadying breath and pivoted to head back inside.

"Where are we going now?" I called, rushing to catch up with him. Maggie hurried beside me.

"The stables. If whatever made Lightspeed drop dead was in the hay, we need to a get closer look."

Vinnie had a determined expression as he led us back down the hall to the entrance of the stables. It felt a little strange to be sneaking around, looking for clues under the law's nose with a lawman at our side. But Vinnie was just a civilian here, like Maggie and me. I couldn't lie that it felt nice having him with us for protection though. Magic could do a lot of things and I'd gotten so much stronger since moving to Brookhaven, but I was not invincible. It was just reassuring to know he had our backs.

We had reached the secured door to the stable and Vinnie tapped a card to the keypad. I spotted Ryan's name on it. "Vinnie, did you lift that from Ryan while you were calling the paramedics?"

"He wasn't going to be using it. Besides, I don't need magic to know something is fishy about this whole thing. Come on, we need to be quick and quiet before the police bring their people in to go over the stables with a fine-toothed comb."

He pulled several pairs of latex gloves from his leather jacket's inner pockets. "Always come prepared."

6

———

I'd done my fair share of sneaking around places I wasn't technically meant to be since moving to Brookhaven. I'd never done it with the blessing of law enforcement. Yet, Vinnie looked all too comfortable as he pulled on the gloves and tapped the keycard to the locking mechanism on the door. I always hated how the gloves made my hands dry out, but I pulled them on any way. We didn't need to leave more prints than necessary for the police to pull.

"So, what do we look for?" I asked as Vinnie walked in a purposeful straight line to the far end of the stable.

"Anything that seems out of place. Something

that might explain why Lightspeed had hay in her teeth. What could have caused her to collapse?"

"This may be a strange question, but how close were Ryan and Lightspeed?" Maggie was half a step behind us.

"What do you mean?" Vinnie glanced over his shoulder before turning back to the stalls in front of him. He slowed his pace as we finally came up to the other jockeys, settling their horses.

"He communed with animals, and you said he was the only one who could handle her. Maybe the magic went deeper than even he realized? Is it possible that he collapsed as a direct reaction to what happened to her?"

"Like a sympathetic attack?" I posed.

"Yeah."

"I mean, I haven't seen him in a decade, but it's possible. To be honest, I don't really know what he would do to keep those skills sharp. He did always have an affinity for Lightspeed even when we were younger."

"Let's hope whatever it was that made her drop didn't get into his system and he'll recover."

The stable felt like it went on forever as we made our way past riders stripping out of their racing gear and freeing their horses from bridles and saddles. A few of the beasts eyed us as we passed, and I couldn't help but feel like they were silently judging me. I shook my head at the absurd thought and picked up the pace.

Finally, we had reached Lightspeed's stall. I could hear the sounds of something scraping the floor and Vinnie reached for his hip, only to remember he wasn't carrying his gun. He looked around, picking up a small rake in his dominant hand before rounding the corner and stepping inside. Maggie and I stopped just short of entering the stall.

A slender man with tight, dark curls bent over the floor, shoveling straw into a bucket. It would have been easier to sense anything amiss if my hands weren't constrained by the gloves, but I wasn't about to take them off. Still, I concentrated on the strands still littering the ground and that same woozy feeling hit me.

"It's in the hay," I told Vinnie in a hushed tone.

"Stop what you're doing!" Vinnie sounded far more commanding than I'd ever heard him.

The man stood up, shovel falling from his hands as he looked at Vinnie. Maybe it was the leather jacket or the imposing posture, but he visibly shook at the sight of my friend. "Please, I was just doing what he told me." He spoke in a heavily accented tone—almost Caribbean.

"Who told you to do what?" Vinnie prompted.

"Mister Reese. He said to come back here and clean up the stall."

"When did he tell you that?"

"Once they took the horses out to the starting gate."

Vinnie still held the rake aloft. I squeezed in beside him, pressing my hand to his forearm. "I don't think this guy knows what's going on."

"How could he not?" Vinnie snapped.

"What is going on?"

Maggie tugged Vinnie's other hand to pull him aside. "Come on, let's see what we can figure out over here. Darcy's got this."

The man eyed me warily, taking note of my latex-gloved hands. "Lightspeed collapsed out of the gate. Ryan's being taken to hospital now, because he collapsed, too."

"No, that can't be true."

"We saw it. Everyone did. The police are taking statements from the crowd. We think something might have happened to Lightspeed on purpose." I gestured towards Vinnie. "Do you know who that is?"

The man shook his head. "Well, that's Vinnie.

He's Ryan's cousin and a policeman. He just wants to make sure his family is okay."

"The announcements .... it doesn't come back here." He pointed to the walls. "Too thick I think."

"It's okay. You didn't know." Being this close to the hay was making my vision start to swim. "Do you think we could step out and have a chat over there? I'm a bit claustrophobic," I lied.

He set the bucket down and followed me out of the stall. Thankfully, there didn't appear to be too many prying ears around. "What's your name?"

"Francois Dubois."

"Was it common for Reese to ask you to muck the stall after the horses went out?"

Francois rubbed his chin. "Not at the start of the day. But yeah, I do what he says because he's the boss, you know?"

"Yeah, I understand. And you don't want to get in trouble."

"Please don't tell him I stopped. Please."

"I won't. But can you think of any reason why he'd ask you to do it now instead of after her races were done?"

"No. But he was very specific. He said I had to clear all of the hay and clean out her feed bucket before Mister Ryan came back with her."

"Did that seem odd to you?"

He nodded. "Thanks so much for talking with me. If the police come through, you need to tell them what you told me. Can you do that?"

Francois's eyes went wide. "Uh, I don't want to talk to them."

I didn't need to hear him say it to understand why he was afraid of speaking with law enforcement. Even from my brief interaction with Sgt. Higgs and his officers, I got the feeling they didn't look too kindly on the immigrant population. "But Ryan was kind to you, right?"

"Oh, yes. He always gave me a bonus during the holidays to send home to my family. Even Mister Reese didn't know."

"Then you owe it to him to tell the truth. I don't think you did anything wrong."

"I hope that Mister Ryan is okay. He is a nice man."

"Me, too."

Francois dusted his hands on the backs of his coveralls and hurried off towards the exit of the stable. I joined Maggie and Vinnie where they stood beside an extra row of saddles and other riding gear. "So, your uncle asked Francois to clean up the hay and Lightspeed's feed bucket before the races started. Normally, he does that after all the races are done."

"Why do I get the feeling he's trying to cover something up?" Maggie said.

"Because you two have been developing your investigative instincts," Vinnie answered. I arched a brow at him. "Ginny isn't the only one who thinks you're becoming something of an amateur detective in your spare time, Darcy."

"I'm not sure how I feel about the town's deputy noticing that."

"Don't worry, I don't think Rick's noticed much. That, or Ginny's convinced him to lay off, because it's better to have an unofficial third hand sometimes."

"You all have become my family and Brookhaven is my home. I'd do anything to keep it safe."

"So, with Francois clearing away potential evidence, that gives us a good place to start," Maggie noted.

"I can tell you whatever was tainting the bit of hay I found in Lightspeed's mouth was definitely all over the stall floor," I said, wiping sweat from my forehead with the back of my gloved hand. "I don't have any idea what it could be, but it was definitely there."

Vinnie looked around the space until he spotted

a metal thermos hanging off one of the pegs near the extra saddles. He pulled it free, unscrewed the lid and dumped the contents—what smelled like day-old coffee—on the ground. "You said he was supposed to clean out the feed, too?"

I eyed the thermos warily. "That's not exactly an evidence bag."

"Right. I have a couple in the seat on my bike." His cheeks flushed with a touch of embarrassment as I called him out for not following proper police procedure.

"Your VIP pass ought to get you back in without issue," Maggie said. "Go grab a bag. We'll stay here and make sure no one gets rid of the evidence."

Vinnie tossed the thermos aside and hurried away from the stall, back the way we'd come. I kept my distance from the hay, my stomach still unhappy with the proximity to whatever it was tainting the hay. Maggie brushed a few curls off my forehead. "You should get some air, too."

"I'm fine. I'm not going to leave you here by your-self. Where you go, I go."

"Do you have any idea what it could be?"

I shook my head. "Just that it messes with my balance and my vision. I touched that bit from her teeth, and it was like I could absolutely feel what she had gone through. The disorientation, the fear."

"Ugh. That sounds horrible."

I gestured to the space around us. "This all feels like someone had to have planned it."

"And Ryan's dad looks like the prime suspect."

"Or at the very least he knows something about what's going on. Especially asking Francois to clean up before the police got a chance to look around the place."

"But what reason could he have for wanting to harm his own horse, or his son?"

"Why do people do anything horrible? For power, or money or revenge? Take your pick."

"I wish we could get him to open up to us."

"If we could get him talking to Ginny, he'd have no choice but to spill the beans," I said with a laugh. In reality, I was only half joking. Her particular type of magic could prove useful in this sort of situation.

Before Maggie could say anything else, footsteps echoed on the metallic flooring, getting louder. I turned to see a woman with a dark braid pressed close to her neck approaching us. She carried a riding helmet under one arm, and she sported a jockey uniform.

"I don't recognize you two," she said, stopping

about a couple meters or six feet from us. She stared like she was trying to commit our faces to memory.

Maggie held up her VIP badge. "We're guests of Ryan, the jockey who collapsed. We were just looking to gather some of his things to take to the hospital."

"Oh, sorry. I didn't think Ryan had anyone here, but his dad."

"Did you know Ryan?" I shoved my hands into my pockets to conceal the gloves.

"We've raced against each other for a few years now. He's a decent guy. Very dedicated to his horse."

"I'm guessing you knew how old Lightspeed was?" She nodded. "Did you think it was strange that they kept racing her?"

"I mean she wasn't as spry as she used to be, but she seemed fine to race. At least we all thought she was. Some people even said she was going to win it all this season. Go out on a high note."

"I'm assuming as a jockey you're not allowed to bet on the races, but did a lot of people have money riding on her winning or finishing in a certain place?" Maggie pressed.

"I'm not sure. It wouldn't surprise me though." She shifted her helmet to the other arm. "I really hope Ryan is okay."

"You were here before the races started, right?" I gave her a hopeful look.

"Yeah, but my stall is quite a ways over there. If you were hoping I saw something that might have provided a clue as to why she fell, I don't remember seeing anything. But I'm sure the police will figure it out."

She had far more hope in the police sergeant than I did. The officer seemed almost disinterested and annoyed at having to come answer the call.

"Thanks anyway ..." I said, pausing with the hope she'd at least fill in her first name.

"Jayka," she replied as if reading my mind.

"Nice to meet you, Jayka."

I spotted Vinnie approaching us at a hurried pace. I could see he had one hand in one of the many zippered pockets of his jacket. At least we had a sneaky way to get the evidence off the premises. And with the handful of local officers taking witness statements, it was unlikely they'd notice us leaving.

"Who's this?" Vinnie stepped around the girl, keeping his pocketed hand out of her line of sight.

"Jayka. One of the other jockeys. She was just telling us she hopes Ryan gets better soon."

"I appreciate that. I'm his cousin," Vinnie explained, offering an ungloved free hand.

She shook it. "Oh, that's right, he did mention something about reconnecting with a cousin. I bet this wasn't how you hoped the reunion would go."

"Not at all." he pulled his hand away. "I noticed a few cameras leading up to the area around here. You wouldn't know who we should talk to about making sure that footage doesn't get deleted? For the police investigation."

" You'd probably have to talk to Karl, the head of security. But if I'm honest, those aren't even on a lot of the time. Just the ones that cover the cash boxes."

"It's worth a try anyway. Karl, you said?"

"Yeah, you can't miss him. He's the one with the ridiculous soul patch on his chin."

I watched Jayka retreat back in the direction of her stall, disappearing from view. Vinnie exhaled and pulled out a clear evidence baggie. He opened it and held it out to me. "Let's get some of the hay and any of the feed that's left."

"Let me do it," Maggie said, snatching it before I could. "You've had enough exposure to this stuff already."

"So, what do we do if Karl doesn't feel like sharing the video footage?" I asked as Maggie set to work.

"We go through as many legal channels as we

can. And if that doesn't work, then we get creative. If someone did this to Ryan, I want them to pay in a court of law."

"We'll figure out who did this."

"Got it," Maggie said in a stage whisper before handing two sealed bags over to Vinnie: one with the hay and the other with the feed. He stowed them in his jacket pocket and led the way back to the hallway that led to the ticketing area and the betting booths.

True to Jayka's word, Karl wasn't hard to find amongst the crowd. He was maybe six feet tall, broad shouldered, and clearly had gone bald. The soul patch on his chin made him look like an aging hippy.

"Excuse me, are you Karl?" Vinnie approached with an outstretched hand.

"Who's asking?"

"I'm with the family of the jockey who collapsed. I'm sure the police have already talked to you, but we have some concerns about what happened during the race. We were hoping you'd be kind enough to share the video footage from today?"

"I'll have to clear that with the owner."

"And who's that?" I asked.

"Drake Gorman."

I must have heard Karl wrong. It sounded like he'd said Drake Gorman—the man who was trying to wine and dine Sage into expanding High Time—owned the racetrack. How much money did the guy have to throw around?

"I'd appreciate it if I could speak with Mr. Gorman, then," Vinnie said coolly.

Karl rubbed at his soul patch for a moment before he pulled the radio off his belt. "Karl for Gorman."

I waited behind Vinnie, watching the security officer stand in awkward silence as he waited for someone to acknowledge his request on the other end of the radio. Finally, the device came to life. "Go for Gorman."

"There's a guy down here, asking about some video footage?"

"Police?"

"Says he's family of the kid who went down on the track."

"Switch to channel six."

Karl stepped back and pulled a different device from his belt, pressing it to his ear. He glanced at us for a moment before saying, "Understood." He attached the radio and the other device to his belt. "Sorry. No can do."

Well, that wasn't overly accommodating. We were going to have to get creative if we wanted to see any of the footage. Not that I had any real sense of what it would reveal. We had no way to know how long Lightspeed had been exposed to the tainted hay or even if it had made her fall. If I had some privacy and Maggie's help, it was possible I could tease out what it was from the hay. I eyed Vinnie's jacket pocket.

"Come on, we should go check on your uncle," I said, tugging my friend by the wrist.

Vinnie looked like he wanted to put up a fight, but Maggie patted his other arm, and he acquiesced. Karl watched us go until we made it to the foot of the stairs that would lead us up to the VIP box.

"You two heard who owns this place, right?" It didn't matter if anyone heard us, but my question still came out in a hushed tone.

"Yeah, that was the man who Sage was meeting with about the dispensary, right?" Maggie replied and I nodded.

"Yeah, that can't be a coincidence."

"That's news to me," Vinnie finally offered. "Back when I was on better speaking terms with the family, Uncle Reese and my dad owned the place outright. Obviously, that's not the case anymore."

"Maybe you should have a chat with your dad?" I suggested.

"I doubt he'd tell me anything. If Ryan were awake, I'm sure I could get him to explain everything I've missed these last few years."

But Ryan wasn't awake as far as we knew. Which meant we needed to get the information from another source.

"I have a feeling if I'm going to get anything from the hay, I'm going to need to do it sooner rather than later."

Vinnie passed me the baggie and I stuffed it in my jacket. It wasn't as neatly concealed as he'd had it, but it would have to do. "Okay, I'll talk to Reese. See what I can learn."

"You sure you want to do that alone? It was pretty icy up there before," Maggie said.

Vinnie tugged his jacket back into place. "I can handle my uncle. Besides, I've got my interrogation skills to fall back on."

"What if he's headed to the hospital already?" I said.

"Then that's where I'll go next. Let's meet back at Ginny's in a couple of hours. Hopefully, one of us will have something to show for it."

As Vinnie started up the stairs, I spotted Francois hurrying through the throngs of people still trying to leave the facility. A man was behind him with an oversized medical bag. They were headed for the track. It hit me then that no one had touched or moved Lightspeed. If she'd died, surely there would be an inquiry of some sort. Perhaps the man with the bag was a vet.

"I'll meet you at the car. I just need to do one thing," I told Maggie, passing the evidence bag to her as discreetly as possible.

To her credit, Maggie didn't ask me what I was about to do. I pushed my way through the crowd until I'd reached the stands. The metal clanged beneath my weight as I rushed towards the track. Like I'd guessed, the man with the bag knelt beside

Lightspeed. He had a stethoscope around his neck and pressed it to her flank. Francois stood off to one side, wringing his hands.

"Hi there," I said, tapping the him on the shoulder.

Francois jumped as he turned to look at me. "You scared me, miss."

"Sorry. I just wanted to ask you one other question, if that's okay?"

He cast a nervous look at the vet still poking and prodding the horse. "Uh, you can ask."

"Who usually fed Lightspeed? I don't know much about horses, but I'm guessing she had to be on a special diet to maintain her racing form?"

"Mister Ryan did most days. Sometimes if he was running late, Mister Reese told me to do it."

"So, no one else touched her feed?"

"No."

"Sorry, one last thing. Did she ever get into the hay in her stall? Like try to eat it or anything like that?"

"No, not that I ever saw."

"Thanks."

I made a mental note to see if Vinnie could find a way to get a copy of the vet report. It might not hurt to get a look at her prior records, too. Though that was probably stretching our luck. I retraced my steps back to the front of the facility and caught Karl eyeing me from his security post. I offered him a small wave before I walked into the parking lot and hurried off to find Maggie's car.

She sat in the driver's seat studying the evidence bag. "Can you describe exactly what you felt when you were holding the hay or near it?" She set the bag in one of the empty cup holders in the center console.

"Woozy. Like I was off balance. My vision went funny, and my heart was racing."

"Hmm. Sounds like a poison of some sort."

"But why poison a racehorse?"

"Like I said, plenty of reasons and none of them good. I think we ought to dig more into our friend Mr. Gorman when we get back."

"Agreed. I'll see what Sage can tell us about him, too." As Maggie put the car in reverse, I looked up and caught movement in the VIP box. We were too far away to see what exactly was going on, but I spotted Vinnie's leather jacket moving about the space.

"This was not what he'd hoped for with a family reunion," I said softly.

"It feels a little strange doing all of this sneaking

around with his blessing," Maggie commented as she joined the flow of traffic back onto the highway.

"Agreed. But in a good way."

"Let's go back to my place. It would be more comfortable and I have a few things I'd like to try to counteract the affects while you're magically snooping around the evidence."

"Sounds good to me."

I rested my head against the passenger side window and watched the cars moving along in the side mirror's reflection. Unlike our trip to the track, Maggie's phone said it was only a half hour drive back to Brookhaven. I thought about looking Drake up on my phone, but the car's engine lulled me into a light doze. Maybe it was the lingering effects of my proximity to the tainted hay, but I wasn't going to fight my body's need to recover.

"Darcy, we're here." Maggie's voice roused me from my nap.

I opened my eyes and found myself staring at the front of her building. I sat up and my neck muscles twinged in protest at the fact I hadn't moved from my original position in so long. Groaning, I undid the seatbelt and grabbed the evidence bag from the center console before following Maggie up to her third-floor apartment.

She rummaged around in the kitchen while I sat down on the couch in the attached living room. I set the clear bag on the table in front of me and rubbed my forehead, trying to puzzle out the pieces of information we had so far.

"Would the type of poison change how long someone might need to expose Lightspeed before they got the desired result?"

"Possibly. I would assume it depends on the dosage and what they were actually hoping to achieve. I mean, for all we know whoever was poisoning her wasn't trying to kill the horse. Maybe they just wanted to make her sick enough that she'd bow out of the races for the rest of the day. I mean you heard Nina, a lot of people thought she was going to win it all this year. I'm sure that made a lot of people unhappy."

"I wonder if there's a way we could check to see who might have held a grudge against Ryan and Lightspeed. They had to beat out someone to make it into the race."

"One thing at a time." Maggie sat down beside me with a large teapot and matching cup. She stirred something into the pot's contents before pouring it out. I could see her hands glowing faintly as she worked, infusing it with her magic. I couldn't deny that I was relieved that she was going to be boosting my own abilities. It always felt easier to access my magic when Maggie was around. Then again, she'd been one of the first people to truly help me to access and understand my magic.

"I want you to drink this before you do anything else. It should help boost your body's ability to fight off the side effects of whatever is in there."

I downed the contents of the cup she offered me before wiping the sweat from my palms. I was more confident in my skills than I'd ever been, yet that didn't stop the nerves from coming to the surface. I reached for Maggie's hand, and I held it tight. "Just in case."

"Whatever you need."

Together, we opened the evidence bag. I picked up some of the feed first, rolling it between my fingers. It made my stomach queasy, but I honestly couldn't determine if it was because it had been poisoned or from it being horse food. I closed my eyes, trying to draw out the hints of plant matter, but it was as if it were completely absent.

Interesting.

I returned the feed to the bag and took a deep breath before picking up the straw. A bitter taste hit my tongue immediately and my temples throbbed. I wanted to put it down, but I didn't dare. It was reacting to my magic somehow and I needed to follow the clue wherever it went for both Vinnie and Ryan's sakes.

Show me what you saw.

I felt my magic surge around me, washing over my body, and pooling in my hand. When I opened my eyes, my vision was strangely distorted. I could see ahead of me and farther behind me than I ought to. Was I somehow seeing through Lightspeed's eyes or the hay? Maggie's apartment had been replaced by the metallic stable and the enclosed stall where Lightspeed stood. She was pawing at the ground, already starting to list to one side. She blew out anxious breaths, but I couldn't quite tell how long she'd been standing in the hay. She wanted to escape, trying to get away from the hay beneath her hooves, but to no avail. It was everywhere.

"There you are," a semi-familiar voice said.

The magic fueling the plant-based memory faltered as Maggie's own spell fought to keep me grounded. Struggling I tried to figure out who had just approached the horse's stall. I did my best to pour more power into my own spell. The surroundings sharpened a little, but so did the taste in my mouth. Something small and white fluttered past the horse's head. I watched her jaws work as whoever had spoken—I was fairly certain it was a man's voice—removed the bridle. He bent down and I caught a glimpse of Reese's face before he stood back up. I heard Lightspeed's teeth chewing something he'd given her before the memory faded.

I sat back against the couch, my chest heaving as I let the hay fall from my fingers. Maggie's hand squeezed mine and warmth flooded my body, beating back the worst of the symptoms. Maggie pressed a cool cloth I hadn't even realized she had to my forehead, wiping away the sweat that had beaded along my hairline.

"Talk to me."

I licked my lips and swallowed a few times to find my voice. "I think it was Reese. Or at least, I think I saw him. He gave something to Lightspeed before the race."

"What was it?'

"I'm not sure. The perspective was all wonky." The image of the white flower falling to the ground and him hunching over to pick something up came to mind. "It tasted bitter. And there was some sort of white flower. I think he might have actually fed it to her. It fell to the floor, so maybe that's why she had hay in her mouth."

"Bitter taste and white flowers ... sounds like it could be hemlock."

Definitely poisonous and possibly cause anyone, let alone a horse, to keel over.

"I think we need to do some digging into Reese and see why he might have been poisoning his prize racehorse," I declared.

"I'm going to let Vinnie know what we found," Maggie said, standing up and releasing her grip on my hand.

I wished she'd stayed though. The lack of physical connection was making me woozy. I took a few slow, deep breaths and it passed. "While you do that, I'm going to run to the B&B and see if maybe Beau fancies a trip back to the track for a look around."

"Careful, Sam might get jealous since he can't tag along."

I had no doubt my ghostly friend would be sullen about not getting to tag along on this one. But that didn't mean he couldn't do some snooping for me while we were away. A few minutes later I reached the B&B to find Tania sitting on the front porch in a heavy shawl. Beau sat perched on her right knee.

"I didn't expect you back so soon," she said before petting Beau's back. "But he did."

'I can help.'

I smiled at the chameleon. "That's what I was hoping to hear." Sam materialized behind Tania, and I looked at him with as serious an expression as I could muster. "You were right. Trouble seems to have found me again. And this time, it put Vinnie in a tough spot. I need you to look around, see what you can find out about Drake Gorman's interest in the dispensary. I have a feeling there's more to it than meets the eye."

8

_I_ made it down the driveway before I realized that my plan to head to the track to use Beau's camouflage had one rather large flaw. I didn't have a ride to get there. Maggie was busy looking into the medical side of things and as far as I knew, Vinnie was still at the track talking to his uncle. Sheepishly, I turned back to Tania.

She already held out her car keys and offered me a knowing smile. "I think you might be missing something. Unless you plan to walk?"

A gust of chilled air blew past, and I shivered from head to toe. "Rather not if I can help it." I took the keys and gave my friend a grateful smile. "I think I'm just a little off kilter from everything that happened today."

"Understandable. Do be careful."

"I always try."

Tania tugged her shawl tighter around her shoulders as she disappeared back inside. Sam still hovered on the porch once the door shut, and he eyed me with a conspiratorial expression. "So, you really think this investor is bad news?'

"I don't know," I answered with a sigh. "It feels too much like a coincidence that he owns part of the track and now he's come looking to expand High Time's business. Something about it just doesn't sit right with me."

He gave me a mock salute. "I'm on it."

I settled into the driver seat of Tania's VW Bug and Beau scampered down my right arm to settle in the passenger seat. The chameleon curled up, tip of tail to nose and closed his eyes. He gave me one slow blink before he shut them. It was impossible for a reptile to snore, but I could swear he gave off that sentiment as I put the car into drive and headed back onto the highway. Given that Beau was napping and the only other creature in the car, I had no one to talk through my thoughts on the case. Not that I had any real explanation for why Reese might have been poisoning his own horse and put his son into the hospital.

Things would have been so much simpler if Vinnie had been on better terms with his family. He might have gotten them to open up more easily. But I couldn't really hold a strained family relationship against my friend. After all, my own relationship with my parents was non-existent. Thankfully, I'd stayed in touch with my Gran and her sister's family here in the States. Like Vinnie, I just wanted to be accepted by the people who were supposed to love me unconditionally.

Perhaps Ryan struggled with that, too? Sure, he had magic, but it certainly sounded like his ability wasn't exactly what his father had hoped for in his son. Maybe Reese had simply intended to disrupt Ryan's abilities? Or had Ryan happened upon his father's poisoning scheme and became collateral damage?

Luckily, the track facility appeared off to my right and I had to focus on making sure I got into the proper lane to exit the highway. It was definitely not wise leaving me spiraling in my own head. I pulled into the parking lot to find it much emptier than when Maggie and I had left earlier. Clearly the police had gotten through taking more statements. Hopefully, they wouldn't protest if they spotted me on the grounds still. I could always claim I was there with Vinnie and was waiting for him. I scanned the lot and found Vinnie's motorcycle still parked in the same spot.

"Right, time to wake up now," I said and prodded Beau's back gently.

He opened one eye and then the other, studying me languidly before hurrying up to perch on my shoulder. I felt his magic ripple as he blended into my shirt and jacket.

"Keep your eyes open, mate," I said softly as I climbed out of the car and headed inside. The fact I still had my VIP badge made it simple to get through the turnstiles. The track itself was sparsely populated now. I could see a few staff moving around the space, picking up bits of detritus in the stands. I thought I spotted someone down on the track near where Lightspeed and Ryan had gone down. Maybe they were trying to collect evidence? At least by now, they'd moved Lightspeed's body from out in the open.

I cast about for where the security office might be, but nothing stood out to me. I knew the stables were off to my right, so I tried going left and found the ticket counters for betting. One of the employees was still sitting behind her little glass partition. I leaned on the edge of the counter and waited for her to notice me.

Finally, our gazes met, and she jumped. "Uh, betting's closed."

"I know, I wasn't looking to place one."

"Oh. Right. Well, then what do you want?"

I gestured to the empty counters around the woman. "Haven't they sent everyone home?"

"Someone had to stay until the money is collected for the day." She sounded bitter about it.

Not that I could blame her. I wouldn't want to be stuck at what was most likely a crime scene. "And you drew the short straw?"

"They say it's because I have the most seniority. I think they all just were too freaked out to stay."

"I hope this doesn't hurt business too much."

"Not like the place has been doing great lately anyway," she muttered. Her eyes went wide as she realized what she'd just told me.

For a moment, I understood what it must be like for Ginny to pull the truth from people. I suspected this woman just needed to unload on someone and I was as good a person as any.

"It seemed like the place was packed earlier. That had to be good for business."

"Only when the top horses run. When it's just the

second string, the seats are hardly filled. If we clear two grand in a day that's a good day."

I stopped myself from asking how much was awaiting pickup now. It was a possible motive for sure, especially if someone knew which horses to target. With what I'd picked up on, it seemed that it could be an inside job if Reese was involved.

"I'm actually looking for someone. Tall guy, leather jacket. He had a VIP badge, too," I said, shifting the conversation. I needed to tell Vinnie what Maggie and I had learned about the hemlock.

"He was up in the VIP booth last I heard. Well, heard is a strong word. There was a lot of yelling and stomping. You couldn't miss it, even with everything going on down here."

"Thanks."

I retraced the path we'd taken up to the VIP booth and found Vinnie sitting alone in the semi-darkness. The lights turning on overhead frightened me when I walked in. It was enough to jolt him to attention, but the tension in his shoulders eased when he saw me.

"Sorry, I didn't mean to scare you," I said as I slid into the seat beside him. I noted he was holding his left hand, and had something pressed to it.

"You two find anything?"

"Pretty sure Reese was poisoning Lightspeed with hemlock. At least that's what I got from the evidence we took from the stable."

"Poisoning?"

I pointed to his hand. "Looks like you might have figured that part out, too?"

He pulled away the rag to reveal bruising on his knuckles and he flexed his hand. "No, this was just from an old dispute."

I arched a disbelieving brow at him. He sagged in the seat. "I may have accused my uncle of not going to the hospital with Ryan. He barely even moved when everything went down. He just told me to stay out of it, because it was a family matter."

I could feel the anger wafting from him and saw the color intensify in his cheeks. I didn't blame him for wanting to slug his uncle for making that sort of comment.

"Well, I was having a chat with one of the girls downstairs who takes bets. She mentioned that when the top horses aren't running, the track didn't do great business. Which makes me think that today might have been a banner day for the cash drop. Could be a possible motive."

"I've left a message for my dad to see if he'll even talk to me about why he sold his stake in the busi ness. I'm not hopeful. I think I'm going to head to the hospital, so that Ryan sees a friendly face when he wakes up. I don't know how I'm going to break it to him that Lightspeed's gone."

"One thing at a time."

He stood and took a step towards the door before he turned back to me. "How'd you get back here?"

"Borrowed Tania's car. If it's okay with you, I want to look around a bit more."

"Just don't get caught. I don't think I can get you out of any trouble with the local law."

I was about to pat Beau on my shoulder and tell him it wouldn't be an issue, but I stopped short of reminding him that I had a reptilian invisibility shield. We might be working on this case side by side, but that wasn't always going to be true. I didn't need him calling me out on snooping under the cover of magic in the future.

"I will be careful. You have my word. I saw the vet come through before we left. I was hoping he might still be around. Or maybe we could get access to Lightspeed's records. See if we can figure out how long this has been going on."

"I'll ask Ryan if he has them when I get to the hospital ... assuming he's awake."

"He wasn't the one being poisoned. I have to

believe it was just a magical reaction, because of his powers. I'm sure he'll be fine."

Vinnie nodded wordlessly as he left the VIP booth. I followed after him a minute or two later, making sure to let the woman at the betting booth see me. That way she could account for my whereabouts if anyone asked. I even made a show of heading for the doors leading back to the parking lot before I whispered to Beau, "Now would be a good time to go unseen."

'Not much time.'

I couldn't be certain if he meant we didn't have long to catch up with the vet or he wasn't able to sustain the spell for long. Either way, I resolved to be quick. Beau's power rippled over me with a rush of cool air down my body and warmth from within. It was always such a strange dichotomy of sensations when he lent me his invisibility.

I held my hands up to my face to be certain I was fully hidden before I returned inside and walked past the betting area. The lone woman still sat there, checking her phone. I didn't know if I was headed in the right direction until I reached a door marked 'Private.' Luckily, someone had stuck a doorstop in it and I could nudge it open far enough to slip inside. It happened to be the security hub. A row of monitors lined the wall opposite the door and tracked different areas of the facility. I spotted the front entrance and something that looked to be a side entryway. There were a few angles of the track itself as well as the hallway that led to the stables. The head of security I'd seen earlier—the one who'd dropped that Drake Gorman owned the place—leaned over a keyboard. He was tapping away at the keys, and I crept closer to get a better view of what he was watching.

Karl had pulled footage from the hallway leading up to the stables. He'd somehow zoomed in, but I could still make out the timestamp in the corner. It was about an hour before the race began. I could see the back of a man's head and when he tapped in at the door and turned slightly, I realized it was Reese. He was carrying something in his left hand that was obscured by the angle of his body. He disappeared into the stables, reappearing about five minutes later empty handed.

He had found evidence that Reese might have poisoned Lightspeed.

I watched in horror as the man tapped a few additional keys, bringing up a dialog box asking if he wanted to delete the footage. He clicked 'Yes,' and it vanished from the screen. I wanted to reach out and throttle the man. How could he have disposed of evidence like that? Unless he was working with Reese in covering his tracks.

On one of the far-left screens I spotted Reese and the man I'd seen come through to examine the dead horse standing in what looked like one of the lower spectators' stands. It caught the security officer's attention, too, because he tapped another few keys and that image came up enlarged on the center screen. He fiddled with a few settings and suddenly the conversation filled the room.

"You know what I'm going to find when I run the tests, don't you Reese?" the vet asked in a deep, somber tone.

"You're going to find nothing. Just like all the other times." Reese was barely two inches from the other man's face. I could see the bruise under his left eye from where Vinnie had struck him. It didn't seem to bother him in the slightest.

"There are police snooping around here. This has gone too far."

"You let me worry about the police. You do what I tell you to do. Unless you don't like being a free man."

The vet took a step back. "I don't know what you expect me to tell them. They're going to want a reason why a supposedly healthy horse just collapsed right out of the gate."

"Then let them wonder. Now, you're going to file the report that says you found nothing suspicious in your exam. Maybe a bit of an enlarged heart or something. Or old age."

The vet rubbed his chin before taking another step away from Reese. "You had no business racing her at her age. That's for sure."

"Don't give me moral crap. Not when you were the one who came to me asking for help. I took care of you. You owe me this."

'Get out now'

I took my own step back from the monitors. It was then that I realized there had a been a tiny red recording icon in the bottom left of the screen I'd been watching Karl's shoulder. Not only was he covering up for his boss, but he was securing evidence of blackmail. Who did he actually work for? I'd come to the track hoping for answers and all I'd come away with was more questions.

9

___

I needed to tell Vinnie what I'd seen. Maybe he could find a way to anonymously pass it on to the police investigating Lightspeed's death. I was just about to leave, backtracking to the parking lot when Karl's phone rang with an incoming call. He scooped it up, pressing it to his left ear, anchored by his shoulder as he spoke. I froze in place, even as Beau's tiny claws dug into my skin as a painful reminder that he'd warned me to get out.

"Yeah boss?" After a beat, he continued. "I've got it. Don't worry about it. They're not going to find anything."

I ached to know who was on the other end of the line. It could have been Reese or Drake Gorman. My mouth was dry as I strained to catch a hint of the caller's identity when they next spoke. If only I'd been able to compel Karl to put the call on speaker phone.

"I've already arranged for things to go back to normal in the morning. It will be like nothing happened. You have my word." The security guard let out a deep chortle. "Because I'm magic, boss."

Magic?

There was every possibility this man was being facetious. But given that a man was laid up in the hospital fighting for his life all because of a magical bond with a horse, I wasn't going to rule anything out.

'Need to go. Not safe.'

Beau's voice echoed in my head as Karl ended the call and tapped a few keys, locking the screens. He pivoted in his chair, and I hurried out of the hub, hoping I didn't make noise as I scurried back to the entrance of the track. My heartbeat slammed painfully against my ribs as I took off at a sprint to the parking lot and Tania's VW Bug. It didn't stop hammering until I was behind the wheel and the track facility's outline was a distant image in the rearview mirror.

Still, as I motored down the highway, I couldn't dispel the feeling that someone was following me. I glanced in the rearview mirror a few times and could swear I spotted a black van weaving in and out of traffic behind me. My fingers wrapped tighter around the steering wheel as I put on a burst of speed, glancing at the mirror again. Except the vehicle had disappeared.

Beau had settled back in the passenger seat, melting into the upholstery. I was halfway back to Brookhaven before I felt calm enough to call Vinnie. I knew he'd be at the hospital checking on Ryan, but he needed to know what I'd found. The line rang five times before going to voicemail.

"Vinnie, it's Darcy. I have something I need to tell you. It's better if it's not in a message. I'm on my way to the hospital, so I'll just tell you when I get there."

I ended the call and pulled off onto the side of the road to input the address for the nearest hospital. There weren't that many options. I thought I'd heard Vinnie say something about the one outside of town. It added another twenty five minutes to my trip.

I was ten minutes into the drive when my phone rang. I scrambled to answer the call and put it on speaker. I looked down long enough to confirm it was Vinnie calling me back.

"Darcy? Are you there?" Vinnie's voice sounded muffled.

"Yes, I'm here. I'm about fifteen minutes from the hospital."

"Your message said you have something to tell me?"

"It's better if I just tell you in person."

"Sounds cryptic."

"I know, sorry. I just ... maybe I am being a bit paranoid, but I can't shake the feeling we need to be careful about what we do next."

At that moment, I looked in the rearview and that black van reappeared. It pulled around a squat blue car directly behind the VW Bug and zipped past. I tried to catch a glimpse of the driver. Except the windows were tinted and they were going a good ten miles faster than me.

"You still there?"

"Yeah. I ... I'll meet you in the lobby."

"Right. See you soon."

I didn't like the way Vinnie sounded, like someone was watching him or listening to him, too. Surely Reese wouldn't be spying on his own nephew, no matter the bad blood between them. Yet, the man had appeared to drug his own racehorse and possibly extorted his own vet to cover it up. For what ... insurance money?

The signs leading to the hospital exit off the highway came into view as I pressed down on the gas, shooting past other cars to get off the main thoroughfare and into the more commercial area. I found the visitor parking at the hospital easily enough and left Beau in the passenger seat.

Swallowing the lump of fear in my throat, I walked into the lobby. Relief washed over me when I spotted Vinnie waiting. He had worry lines creasing his forehead as he approached.

"What couldn't you tell me on the phone?"

"Is there somewhere private we can go?"

"Come with me."

Vinnie led me to a bank of elevators and hit the up button. I cast him a curious look, but he remained silent as he waited for the doors to open. The elevator on the far left dinged and the doors slid open. Vinnie guided me inside and hit a button for the third floor. The doors slid shut and we began to move upward. We were almost to the second floor when he reached over and pulled a switch, stalling the elevator.

The sudden stop made my stomach lurch. "Isn't this illegal?"

Vinnie patted his pocket, and I realized he'd stopped to get his badge. "Talk to me, Darcy."

"So, I went back to the track. I don't know what I was hoping to find, but there is definitely some sort of cover-up going on. I watched that security guard we talked to delete footage showing your uncle going into and out of the stables right before the race. I saw Reese carrying something on the footage too. He fed something, a white flower, possibly hemlock to Lightspeed."

"You think he poisoned her? That bastard."

"It's possible. What do you know about that security guard, Karl?"

"Nothing. It's been so long since I was around the track, most of the people working there are different. But I can do some digging into the guard."

"Also, he recorded some footage of your uncle talking to the vet who came to examine Lightspeed. It sounded like your uncle was threatening the vet. Like they'd done something like this before. The vet didn't seem very keen to help him."

"I knew my uncle was a manipulative prick, but threatening people never seemed to be part of his game."

"And there's something else. The guard got a call from someone who sounded like they were in charge. He called them boss. He said that things would be open tomorrow like nothing had ever happened. And the police wouldn't find anything."

"Boss? You mean Uncle Reese?"

I shrugged. "Maybe Mr. Gorman? I couldn't hear both sides of the conversation. I just thought I should tell you. I don't know ... maybe you could call in a tip to the police who are investigating?"

Vinnie let out a snort. "I've had Rick look into them for me. His assessment wasn't exactly glowing. They tend to close investigations and cases with as little work as possible. Taking all those witness statements was probably the most work they've done in months."

"I hate to ask, but could the police be tied into whatever's happening at the track? I'm obviously no expert, but they did look rather annoyed about having to respond to the call."

Vinnie rubbed the stubble on his chin. "I wouldn't put it past them to at least be turning a blind eye. Like I said, according to Rick they're known for pretty lazy work."

"That means we just need to be extra thorough."

"I appreciate your help on this, Darcy. I know I shouldn't have involved you, but I am glad to have you on my side."

I gave him a conspiratorial wink. "I think we both know there was no stopping me from snooping, not when my friends are concerned."

"I keep telling Rick we ought to just deputize you."

"Oh, I'm not sure I'm ready for that sort of responsibility. The odd case here or there, I'm happy to lend a hand. But being official, that seems so formal." I gestured to the switch he'd flipped to halt the elevator's progress. "I think we ought to get going. We don't want people to worry that you've hijacked the lift."

Vinnie offered up a sheepish grin before toggling the switch again. The elevator resumed its upward progress, finally letting us off on the third floor. After exiting, we received some nasty looks from the staff as we headed down a corridor to the right. I wasn't sure where we were heading, but Vinnie appeared to know his way around.

"Have you had any luck getting in touch with your family about what happened for them to sell their share in the track?"

"Still working on it." Vinnie's voice was hushed, his jaw hardly moved when he spoke.

I let the subject drop for now. When we stopped walking, I realized we were outside a private room. I spotted Ryan's name on a whiteboard outside the room with a small R marked beside it.

"Oh, good you're back," a nurse with a deep complexion said, flagging Vinnie down.

"Has something happened?" Vinnie failed to hide the concern in his tone.

"The doctor wanted to speak to you. You're Ryan's family, right?"

"Yes, I am."

She pointed to a tall man with a white coat over dark blue scrubs approaching from the far end of the hall. "He'll be right in to speak with you, sir."

Vinnie pushed into the room. Inside there were two beds. One was empty, the blankets tucked neatly in along both sides of the mattress. The sterile room made me shiver. All I could picture was this must be how it looked after someone had died.

Don't be so dramatic, Darcy.

They probably just had someone discharged and remade the bed, so it was ready for the next patient. I turned my attention to the bed on the far right. That must be what the little R meant on the board outside so that the nurses and doctors could identify the patients on each side of the room more easily. Ryan lay in the bed, his eyes closed with a cannula stuck up his nose and the tubes looped around his ears.

"He was on an oxygen mask before," Vinnie said quietly.

"That must mean he's improving. Have they said anything else about his condition?"

"Just that they were waiting on some lab results."

A knock at the door cut the conversation short as the doctor entered, tucking a folder beneath his arm. He stopped briefly at a hand sanitizing station, taking a few squirts of disinfectant before he crossed the space to us. He gave me a skeptical look.

"She's with me. anything you need to say about Ryan, you can say in front of her," Vinnie said, interpreting the doctor's look in the same manner I had.

"Well, preliminary tests didn't show any signs of infection or an underlying condition that might have caused him to collapse today. But we did find trace amounts of hemlock in his blood."

"That's poison," I blurted.

"It was likely a recent exposure. Nothing huge, but we think it explains the reason he collapsed."

At least in part. The doctor couldn't know about Ryan's connection to Lightspeed. Part of me feared that Ryan somehow knew that his beloved mare was dead, and he was still unconscious because he didn't want to deal with the heartbreak. But he needed to know what was going on.

"When will he wake up?"

"That's up to Ryan. We've flushed the hemlock from his system. Nothing medical is keeping him from regaining consciousness. I do think it is a good sign we weaned him down from such heavy oxygen. But I think right now, you need to be patient."

Vinnie didn't look pleased with the explanation, but he didn't argue. He turned to look at his cousin and reached out to grip Ryan's left hand in his right. "I'm here, Ry. I'm here."

I settled in one of the oversized chairs by the window and watched as Ryan's chest rose and fell slowly in time with the monitors keeping track of his vitals.

"Has anyone else been to see him?" I looked at the doctor.

"I honestly can't say. One of the nurses might know."

"Thank you," Vinnie said and the doctor left the room.

"It seems awfully callous of Reese not to come visit his son in the hospital. For all he knows, Ryan could be in a coma, or on life support."

"Their relationship has been strained from what Ryan implied earlier. I'm not shocked Reese isn't here. If he's been dosing Lightspeed with hemlock like you proposed, maybe he'd been doing the same thing to Ryan to try and keep him quiet."

As I studied the man in the bed, a thought occurred to me. "What if he hasn't woken up yet, because there is still some hemlock in his system?"

"It's possible I suppose. It's not like they can monitor it in real time. What are you thinking?"

"It's a long shot. I mean I don't even know if this would work, but if it's active, maybe my magic could find it and snuff it out."

"You could do that?"

"Won't know unless I give it a try."

I usually encouraged plants to grow and thrive. It's all I'd focused on, cultivating with my magic since I'd come to Brookhaven. But that didn't mean I couldn't have the opposite effect. I moved to sit beside Ryan on the bed and took both of his hands in mine. Closing my eyes, I envisioned my magic blossoming in my mind's eye. I felt it take root within my core, pulsing through me ready to obey my every whim.

Next, I pictured the hemlock flowers in my mind's eye. I zeroed in on the way they'd made me feel, the woozy sensation. Focusing on the danger they posed.

'Seek it out.'

I tightened my grip on Ryan's hands as my fingers warmed. In the blink of an eye, I could see tiny tendrils of the plant's poison still in Ryan's body. I opened my eyes to find a hazy white sheen over his chest. "It's still in there," I said, feeling sweat prickle along my hairline.

'Snuff it out.'

I imagined the tiny seeds of the hemlock's power shriveling and decaying to dust. Slowly, the sheen dissipated from above Ryan's body. I relinquished my grip on his hands and sunk back against the bed.

"Did it work?" Vinnie's voice was hushed.

Ryan gave a cough that shook his whole body. It was followed by another cough and the cannula came loose, slipping down to his upper lip. He blinked, his eyes glassy and unaware of his surroundings. He shut his eyes again and tried to take a steadying breath. Vinnie eased a cup of water into his cousin's hands. Ryan opened his eyes again, his gaze still unfocused as Vinnie guided the cup to his lips and he drank. He managed to ask with a raspy voice, "Wh-what happened to Lightspeed?"

Vinnie patted the man's knee through the hospital blankets. "I'm sorry, Ryan. Lightspeed's gone. And it looks like there's been foul play."

10

———

Ryan's gaze zeroed in on Vinnie. Confusion and disbelief took over his expression and yet I could also see a hint of resignation. A part of him had to have known that his horse was gone. He struggled to sit up in the bed and Vinnie was at his side, easing him up against the pillow.

"I could feel something ... off," Ryan began, his voice gruff. "I can usually sense distinct emotions from her. This was just a jumble of things. Some times I wish I could actually read her mind."

"We think she was poisoned," I explained.

"What? How?"

I cast Vinnie a glance, asking his permission to share what Maggie and I had uncovered. I had no doubt that Ryan was a victim in all of this. Yet, I didn't want to set him back in his recovery by bringing up that it appeared his father was in part responsible for what had happened with Lightspeed.

"We have reason to believe that someone was lacing her feed with something over a long period of time," Vinnie answered. "We were able to get a small sample. Maggie and Darcy did a little digging."

Ryan's brow furrowed. "What? Is that legal?"

Vinnie cleared his throat. "Not exactly, no. But I wasn't going to leave anything to chance. Not with who's investigating."

Ryan let out a bitter laugh. "Yeah, talk about corrupt police." Ryan looked over at me. "Can you tell me what you found?"

"We're pretty sure it was hemlock. I found some flowers in her stall and that's what our research pointed to as well. I think given her age and how much she'd been pushed while being dosed, it was only a matter of time until something like this happened. I'm so very sorry."

"There were only a few people who could have been lacing her feed," Ryan said, rubbing at his forehead, the pulse monitor bumping against his brow.

"You let us worry about that. We just want you to rest up," Vinnie insisted.

"Can you remember what happened right before you collapsed?" I settled on the very edge of the bed. "We all saw her go down, but you stood up for a minute before you fell."

Ryan closed his eyes and pressed his lips together. "I remember this weird wave of panic washing over me. Maybe it was her fear. And then this overwhelming sense of dizziness and everything went black."

"That sounds terrifying."

Voices grew louder in the hall outside of Ryan's room. I couldn't say why, but I had the sense that our time to get any other information from Ryan was running out. "Can you think of anyone who might want to harm your family specifically? A rival or anything?"

Ryan shook his head. "I don't think so."

"What about the new owner, Mr. Gorman? Any reason he might want Lightspeed out of the race?"

"He's hardly around. Comes by maybe once a month or so. He doesn't even stay for the races. Thought it was kind of weird he'd be invested in a track and not want to spend time there or even try to understand the business."

The more I heard about Mr. Gorman, the more I disliked him. I filed the information away for later reflection.

"You rest up, Ryan."

I nodded my head towards the door, catching Vinnie's eye as I did so. He glanced over his shoulder before he stood up and gave Ryan's right hand a pat. "Stay strong, Cuz. We're going to figure out who's behind this. You have my word."

I was partway to the door when I pivoted around. "One other thing I should probably mention. You had traces of hemlock in your bloodstream. It was keeping you unconscious. Any chance you came in contact with her contaminated feed?"

"I don't know. Maybe?"

Vinnie tugged on my arm and guided me out of the room. I spotted the doctor who'd spoken with us down the far end of the hall in conversation with a tall man. There was just enough time to confirm it was Reese before Vinnie pulled me more forcefully out of sight.

"So, what's our next move?" I pressed as we descended to the lobby.

"I'm going to loop Rick in, see what he can do. I don't trust the locals to actually investigate."

"I wish I'd found a way to record what I'd seen Karl do with the security video."

"Maybe I ought to send Rick to have a chat with Uncle Reese. Use a little of that supernatural charm of his to shake the truth loose."

By charm, I suspected he meant the added strength and agility of turning into a wild cat afforded only by Brookhaven's Chief of Police. The shaking part, I could only guess he didn't mean it literally. At least I hoped he didn't mean it literally.

"Is there a way we could see what the other jockeys are saying about what happened? If one of them was involved, maybe that would give us a different way to come at your uncle."

Just then, my phone buzzed with an incoming call from Maggie. I answered it on the second ring. "Hi, you."

"Can you come back to my place?"

"You find something?"

"It's better you come back, and I explain in person."

It wasn't like Maggie to be so paranoid. Still, I wasn't about to argue with her. "Be there in like fifteen minutes."

"Stay in touch," Vinnie told me as he held the door open for me.

After returning the car to the B&B, I walked into Maggie's apartment to find my girlfriend and my landlady waiting for me with Sam. He bobbed just behind the couch. I eased the door shut behind me. "Why do I get the feeling I'm in trouble?" I handed Tania the car keys.

Maggie rushed me and pulled me into a tight embrace, planting a kiss on my lips. "I was worried about you."

"I was with Vinnie. Nothing to worry about."

"You asked us to look into Drake and keep an eye out for him," Sam reminded me. "You're not going to like what we found."

My stomach did an uncomfortable flip as I allowed Maggie to lead me to the kitchen table where her laptop sat open.

"I was able to do some digging into his background," she began, tapping away at the keys to reveal financial reports and bank statements on the screen. "He comes from serious old money back in Australia. But he's been in the States for about ten years."

"That's not nefarious."

"No, but it seems that every venture he gets into

sees a small surge in profit before it absolutely tanks."

"So, he's not very smart with his money then?"

"He talks a good game, but he bails when things take a nosedive."

"I trailed him to the pier," Sam jumped in. "He was on the phone with someone a while ago. Sounded like he wants to make sure the track is up and running tomorrow."

Well, that confirmed the identity of the mystery caller I'd overheard Karl speaking with. "That doesn't necessarily mean he purposely killed a prized racehorse."

"But if he is such a poor businessman, then where does he get the funds to keep investing in new ventures?" Tania pointed out.

"Maggie said he was rich back home. Maybe he's got accounts there that he can pull from?"

"The exchange rate isn't strong. He wouldn't risk that," Maggie answered. "There's something else going on."

"Well, I am almost certain Reese had something to do with it. Whether he had intended to hurt Ryan in the crossfire is still up in the air. But the way they interacted, I wouldn't put it past him."

"Not to play devil's advocate, but are we sure that

Reese is really the mastermind? What if someone ... I don't know, forced him?" Maggie suggested.

"Like whom?"

"Maybe a competitor? Someone who was tired of them always having a winning horse."

"Ryan couldn't think of any rivals when Vinnie and I talked to him at the hospital just a bit ago."

Maggie wiggled her fingers and leaned over the computer once more. "He had also just woken up from being unconscious and suffering a trauma. Maybe he wasn't thinking straight."

She turned the laptop to face me, and I could see Ryan's social media profiles. Even though Maggie wasn't friends with him, and I could see that Ryan had set his accounts to private, we had full access to the page.

"Sometimes I forget you're a part-time hacker," I said, sitting beside her.

"Vinnie ought to change his passwords more frequently," Maggie answered, moving the cursor to reveal we were viewing the profiles from Vinnie's account.

"Oh, he's going to right pissed with you when he finds out."

"Let's be honest, right now Vinnie isn't exactly acting within the bounds of the law."

"Well, let's see what we can find out before he realizes what you've done."

Tania moved to stand behind us as Maggie scrolled through Ryan's page. There were copious numbers of photos with him and Lightspeed showing off medals and ribbons over the years. A few pictures were of Ryan with Reese looking moderately impressed by his son's performance.

"This all looks normal," I noted as Maggie went back a good six months.

"What about those comments?" Tania said, pointing to a photo of Ryan posing for something captioned Region's Rising Stars. Another horse and jockey were at the far right of the photo, as if someone had intentionally cropped them out.

Maggie clicked the photo to expand the comment section. One name popped up multiple times in the conversation—Jayka Perez. I could see from her profile picture that she was in a riding outfit, complete with helmet. I looked closer and realized she was the helpful jockey Maggie and I had run into earlier. The nature of her comments were certainly inflammatory and unkind towards Ryan. And written in all caps.

"Ryan didn't reply to any of them," Maggie noted.

"No, but it looks like someone did and then deleted the comments. or the platform blocked them," I noted.

"This girl really doesn't like our boy," Sam commented as he materialized in the center of the kitchen table. "Looks like she had reason to want him out of the way, because he was soaking up her spotlight."

It certainly sounded like she had an axe to grind with Ryan and his success. But in the stable earlier why was she so helpful and concerned about Ryan? And it didn't explain why I'd seen Reese feeding Lightspeed the flower or why Karl had deleted that footage and kept the recording of him extorting the vet.

I turned to Maggie. "Do you think you could get

into her account and see what we can find out about her?"

"I need to head to the clinic to do some inventory, but I'll see what I can find out while I'm there."

Next, I looked at Tania. "If you have some time, maybe you could stop by the hospital and chat with Ryan about processing his loss? I suspect he will feel it more deeply than anyone else. He could use someone who has a similar power to help him."

"And I can keep an eye on him," she added.

"There is that too, yeah."

"What about you?"

"I think there's something more to Gorman that we're missing. I'm going to see what I can find at High Time. See what sort of offer he'd made Sage, maybe figure out where the money is coming from."

"Be safe," Maggie said, reaching over to squeeze my hand.

"I will."

Tania and I descended the stairs to the street level, parting ways at the doorway. I watched my landlady head toward the B&B, and I made the short trip to High Time. The front lights were on, and a few cars dotted the parking lot. But when I walked in through the employee entrance, the kitchen was empty. Unease twisted my gut as I walked through the break room to Sage's office. I expected my boss to be there, but she, too, was absent.

Trying to banish the unease from my mind, I made a quick stop in the grow room to check on the plants. I wasn't on shift, but I needed the familiarity of the plants to center me. I breathed in the familiar scent of earth and fertilizer. The hum of the lights overhead was calming and when I bent over a few of the seedlings, the leaves turned in my direction, opening up as wide as they could.

"I'm happy to see you, too," I said, stroking the tip of one of the leaves.

"You always talk to the plants?" a semi-familiar male voice asked.

I stood fast and spun to find Drake Gorman standing in the doorway leading to the break room and the kitchen. My heart hammered in my throat, robbing me of my voice. What was he doing here without Sage? Or anyone around for that matter?

"Uh," I managed. "S-Sometimes. It helps."

"You always come in at odd hours?"

"I'm not working today ... I just ... " He took a step closer. I backed up to maintain distance and my hip bumped into the table behind me.

He let out a laugh. "Relax, I'm not your boss. Yes. So, your secret's safe with me. But if you're going to sample the product, you might want to be a bit more discreet about it."

"I'm not sampling anything. I just wanted to check on the plants," I explained, suddenly feeling extremely protective over the greenery around me.

He gave an exaggerated wink. "Right. Just checking up on them. You know, I have to admit you've got a nice little set up. Hardly anyone else comes in here. You could be taking all sorts of things, and no one would be the wiser. Might need to change that."

"I swear, I'm not taking anything," I protested, gesturing around at the empty space. "Where's Sage and everyone else?"

"On an extended lunch break. My treat."

"And why are you here all alone, then?"

"Just getting better acquainted with everything."

"But, like you said, you aren't my boss. Sage wouldn't agree to let you wander around unchaperoned."

"Well, she did."

The way he looked at me warned that it was the end of the discussion. I wasn't going to be able to snoop with him around. So, I straightened up and pointed to the space behind him. "Well, I'm just going to go then. I actually realized I'm late to meet a friend."

"You do that."

I hurried past him before pausing at the entrance to the break room. "You must be a really good businessman." The words slipped out.

"In fact, I am. But why would you say that?"

"Taking on a dispensary franchise on top of running a racetrack. You're able to balance a lot of different interests."

He didn't have time to answer before my phone vibrated in my pocket. He made a 'take it' gesture. I stepped through the break room to the kitchen and answered the call from Tania.

"You won't believe what just happened—" I said.

"Ryan's fallen into a coma." Tania interrupted.

11

Much like I'd felt earlier when Karl had shared the fact that Drake was part owner of the track, my mind had trouble processing Tania's words.

"What? Say that again?"

"I got here, and the nurse told me that they had to move him into intensive care, because he'd slipped into a coma."

My heart pounded against my sternum as her words finally sank in. "But he was fine when Vinnie and I left. There had been some lingering effects of the hemlock, but I'd cleared it out. He was awake and talking."

"I wish I had more information. Obviously, they

couldn't tell me anything else, given that I am not family."

"Did you notice if anyone else had been there to see him? His dad maybe?"

After a pause on the other end of the line, she continued, "Not that I saw. But they could have been in the ICU with him. What are you thinking, Darcy?"

A horrible thought was taking root in my mind. But I wasn't about to voice it with Drake so close by. I hurried out of High Time and back onto the street. My feet carried me down to the boardwalk. It was sparsely populated with people walking along the water. A few vendors had opened up their stalls, but it was fairly deserted.

"When Vinnie and I were leaving, I saw Reese. He spoke to Ryan's doctor. I couldn't tell what they were saying, but he was definitely there."

"And you think he somehow put his son into a coma?"

"The man isn't exactly what I'd call sentimental. I got the sense he thought Ryan's abilities were weak, not manly enough. And I have to believe he suspected that Ryan sensed something was off with Lightspeed before the race started. Maybe he dosed Ryan again or somehow convinced the doctor that Ryan needed to be sedated. Either way, I don't believe for a second he wasn't involved in some manner."

"For a father to be so callous to his son is heart-breaking. I'm sorry I couldn't be of more help to him."

Tania couldn't. But Maggie might. She'd established some relationships with the hospital staff last year when she'd shadowed rounds. Granted, the doctor she'd been working with had turned out to be a vampire who murdered people in a twisted bid to save his own father's life. Quite the opposite to our current situation.

"I'm going to see if there's anything Maggie can do."

"I know you want to help him and Vinnie. But as good as Maggie's skills are, she can't fix everything," Tania reminded me.

"I know. But I also know she'd never forgive herself if she didn't at least try."

The line was quiet for a moment as I walked along the pier. The sound of the water lapping against the pilons was rhythmic and calming.

"There's something else on your mind."

"I went to High Time, hoping to talk to Sage; or at least take a look through her paperwork from Drake. But no one was there. I mean no one, I went into the grow room and Drake just showed up. He accused me of trying to steal product."

"That's absurd."

"I know. But the fact that he was there and claimed to have convinced Sage to give everyone an extended lunch. It didn't sit right with me. And why would he invest in companies only for them to plummet soon after? What does he get out of it?"

"I don't know. Maggie was looking into that other jockey. I don't think she's found anything yet."

On cue, my phone beeped with an incoming text from Maggie.

Found something. Meet me at Ginny's ASAP.

"Actually, it looks like she's got something." I ended the call with Tania, pivoted on my heel, and headed back to the cafe. I arrived just as Maggie approached from the other side of the street. She spotted me, darted across, and grabbed my arm. She dragged me out of view of the front windows.

"What's gotten into you?" I tried to look over her shoulder. She was clearly trying to block my view of something. Or someone.

"So, I managed to do a little bit more digging into Jayka and I found some messages between her and Drake. It looked like she was his way in ... to the track."

"How so? What do you mean?"

"According to her, Reese wasn't shy about placing bets on his own races. And he wasn't exactly what one might call a good gambler."

"So, he was losing money? But if he was betting at his own track, surely he wasn't in debt to anyone besides himself?"

"All I know is Drake slid into Jayka's DMs and asked about investing in the track. He'd heard there was some discord between the previous owners."

Reese and Vinnie's dad.

"So, you think that Drake came to bail Reese out of debt? But that doesn't explain why Reese would doctor the vet reports or drug his own prize horse."

"I'm guessing he wasn't always betting through the track itself. It's easy to place bets through outside bookies. And some of those people aren't exactly forgiving of late repayments."

"But if his prize horse dies and it's ruled an accident, he could get the insurance money. Because there's no way he wouldn't have taken out a policy on her."

"That's what I'm thinking."

"How would Jayka even know that?"

Maggie hooked her thumb towards the front

window of Ginny's cafe. "Why don't we ask her ourselves?"

"Please tell me you didn't catfish a total stranger to try and solve a case," I pleaded.

"Does it count as catfishing if I roped Vinnie into the conversation, too?"

"I'm sure he'll be happy to hear what she has to say." I caught sight of Vinnie approaching from the direction of the station. He'd left the leather jacket and shades behind, having changed into his deputy uniform. "Tania called me. Ryan slipped into a coma."

"I thought you said he was doing better."

"Something feels off about that, Maggie. I was hoping you might be able to use some of your hospital connections to see him and figure out what might be going on?"

"I'll see what I can do."

I gave Maggie a kiss on the lips, and she stepped aside. Vinnie spotted us and tipped his hat. "Remind me to change my log in information on my social media," he muttered, giving Maggie a knowing look.

"Understood," she said solemnly. "I'm going to see what I can do for Ryan."

She hurried off leaving Vinnie and I to head into

the cafe by ourselves. As the door closed behind us, I scanned the patrons seated throughout the space. Ginny was in her customary spot at the center counter. She held an oversized cup in her hands and her stool swiveled at the sound of the bell overhead. She caught sight of us and gave us a small nod to indicate a dark-haired woman seated alone at a booth in the back.

"You heard about Ryan?" It came out as a question.

"Let's focus on what we can control," Vinnie replied through gritted teeth.

Clearly, he was struggling to keep it together right now.

"I can talk to her by myself if you want. We seemed to hit it off at the stable."

"No. I need to be there for this. Besides, she was helpful before. And I want to know why she was so hostile to Ryan online."

I let Vinnie take the lead as we made our way around the counter and to the back booth. Jayka looked up from her coffee cup and a small bowl of fruit. Either she was too upset to eat more, or she hadn't quite decided on dinner. As it was, my stomach burbled with hunger reminding me I'd been running full steam since the morning. As I sat down across from Jayka, I realized that Ryan's accident took place only a few short hours ago.

My adrenaline had been pumping full tilt and I was only just now starting to come down. It didn't feel like everything could have happened so quickly, and yet here we were. Vinnie squeezed into the booth beside me and held out a hand to the woman. "Jayka, we met earlier, at the stables. I'm Ryan's cousin, Vinnie."

She shook his hand. "Yeah, I remember. I didn't realize you were with the police."

"I'm a police officer here in Brookhaven. Given my connection to Ryan, I've had to do some digging into things ... off book." He motioned to me. "Darcy's been helping."

"I wanted to go to the hospital, but I figured they were only allowing family to see him so far." She studied her cuticles for a moment. "Do they have any idea what happened?"

"Well, actually we're pretty sure someone was poisoning Lightspeed and might have decided to keep Ryan quiet," I blurted.

That got the other woman's attention. "Poison? Seriously?"

"Looks that way," Vinnie confirmed. "You were very helpful back at the track, but we noticed you and Ryan didn't get along online. You made some pretty aggressive comments on some of his posts."

I glanced at Vinnie, arching a brow. I guess Maggie must have filled him in on what had led us to take a closer look at Jayka in the first place.

"Yeah, well, I put a lot into racing and despite what you might think, it's still a male dominated sport. It felt like he was getting all this recognition just because his dad owned the track ... and I let him know that."

"So, you didn't want his horse to die?"

"God no! I mean, Lightspeed was a beautiful horse. And in her prime, she deserved a lot of the accolades she got."

"And now?"

"She's old and not as spry as she used to be. Yet they kept racing her. After some of those social media posts, Ryan and I had a sit down. We cleared the air. I got the feeling he wasn't happy about her racing still, either. But he wasn't going to let anyone else ride her. He said she didn't trust anyone else."

I considered her words for a moment. I couldn't decide whether she believed Ryan was just being protective or if he had deeper reasons for not wanting anyone else to ride Lightspeed.

"What can you tell us about Drake Gorman and

his interest in the track?" Vinnie shifted the conversation, pulling out his notepad and pen, going full police mode.

"He came in a few months ago. Reese's gambling wasn't a very well-kept secret. So, when I heard that some rich guy was looking to invest, I figured maybe he could help Ryan and his family out. Like I said, he and I had cleared the air and were becoming friendly. I knew Ryan's uncle wanted out. He was tired of Reese's debts constantly falling on the business. I thought it was a good thing when he was able to sell his interest in the place."

The way her voice grew softer as she spoke suggested she'd come to regret that decision. Vinnie leaned in, picking up on the change in her tone, too.

"Was Victor involved in the gambling at all?"

"Uh, not that I know of. You'd have to ask him."

"But if Drake came in and bought out Victor's share, how would that help Reese?" I fixed Vinnie with a confused expression.

"Because knowing my father, he'd have given Reese a one-time loan ... with no need to repay it, just to try and get him on the straight and narrow. He probably knew it wouldn't work, but once he was out of there, he likely wouldn't look back."

"I'm sorry, Vinnie. That's harsh."

"And you wonder why I came here?" he murmured.

"Look, I don't live too far from the track. Ryan and I would meet up sometimes to train and let the horses goof off a bit. Since Gorman became a shareholder, I've seen some shady looking guys snooping around the place when it's closed to the public."

"Could you describe them?" Vinnie had his pen in hand again.

"Just kind of sketchy types. Sunglasses, hoodies. Honestly, they looked almost homeless."

"Did you notice if anyone else was around? Drake or Reese?" I could hear a hint of desperation in Vinnie's tone.

"No, but Karl was there. He might have chased them off."

"Thank you for talking to us," I said. "I'm sure it wasn't easy to get involved."

"Yeah, well, I never wanted Ryan out of the game and especially not like this."

"One last question," Vinnie said, pen poised against his paper. "Did you and Ryan use the same vet?"

"Yeah, why?"

"Because we have reason to believe he was

covering things up for Reese in an effort to get Lightspeed to be race worthy longer."

Jayka's face clouded with anger, turning her cheeks a deep beet red color. "That explains it."

"Sorry?" I leaned forward, elbows propped on the table. "Explains what?'

"About a week ago, Ryan called me, because he thought something was off with Lightspeed's vet reports. He'd had some tests ordered just to make sure she was okay and when he read me the results, I thought it was strange because my horse had the exact same results about two weeks ago. Like down to the decimal points."

Vinnie stowed his pen and pad before he stood up. He offered Jayka his hand one more time before he gestured for me to follow him. I gave the woman a small wave before I followed after the deputy. The speed with which Vinnie beat a retreat out of the cafe and back towards the police station signaled he was onto something.

"Want to fill me in?" I called, jogging to keep up with him.

"The vet is dirty. And if he submits that report saying there was nothing abnormal about the blood work and his postmortem exam, Reese is going to get a big payout. It will stave off the bookies for a while, but it won't stop him from doing it again with some other horse."

"Can you pressure the vet?"

"It's not technically my case. I've got Rick's support, but there's only so much he can do to protect me."

"I'm guessing he wouldn't believe that you were there to pick up some records for Reese as a favor," I sighed.

"No, I don't think so. And we don't have time to get him to willingly let us look at those records and prove they were fraudulent."

"From the video I saw, the one that Karl kept, the vet seemed unhappy about going along with the plan. Maybe it wouldn't take much to push him over the edge to flip?"

"I'll see what I can do. For now, I think you should go home and get some rest. You've done everything you can. I truly appreciate it, Darcy."

I would go home, but I doubted I'd get much rest. Vinnie's hands might be tied, but I was going to find a way to shed light on the corruption at the track. No matter what it took.

12

I made it back to the B&B to find Tania setting the table for just the two of us. Plates piled high with chicken breast and roasted vegetables made my mouth water. I sat down and didn't bother waiting for her to join me as I dug in. The seasoning was perfect and eating kept the exhaustion at bay just a little longer.

"So, find anything useful out from that other jockey?" Tania poured a glass of wine and handed it to me. I fixed her with a surprised look, but accepted the glass.

"It sounded like she and Ryan were working through their differences. She put Drake in touch with Vinnie's dad Victor, because she thought it might help Reese's gambling problem. I have a feeling that really didn't help. She also said she saw some shady guys hanging around the track."

"You should probably warn Sage that Mr. Sexy Accent had people poking around today at High Time," Sam chimed in, appearing partway through the wall that divided the kitchen from the dining room. I could only see his torso but it sparkled in a vivid green blazer.

"What do you mean poking around?" I prompted, setting the wine glass down.

"You told me to follow him and so I did. He had some guys wandering around, looking at stuff. Talking about things like safes."

"Well, if he's investing in the property, surely he would want to be sure it was secure," Tania offered.

"No, I got this strange vibe from the guy when I ran into him earlier," I took a bite of the chicken and vegetables, chewing in contemplation. "I think we're missing something about him. It still doesn't make any sense that he keeps investing in these businesses only for them to go under."

"Maybe he just doesn't know how to pick 'em?" Sam offered with a shrug, sparkles from the blazer somehow rubbing off on his translucent cheek.

"There is little else you can do today. You have been running around all day. You need rest," Tania chided. "And a good, hot meal should help. Now eat."

Sam disappeared from view, and I turned my attention to the food in front of me. I definitely didn't say it enough, but Tania was an amazing cook. I was grateful to have her in my life. No doubt without her culinary skills my wallet would be much lighter, and I'd be subsisting on ramen and take-out.

I savored every bite of the meal and let the wine give me that heady feeling I often got after a few drinks. It made me just a touch light-headed and sleepy. Somehow, I knew that Tania understood this was exactly what I needed to quiet my mind and get some sleep.

"Let me help with the dishes at least," I protested when Tania shooed me away from the sink twenty minutes later.

"I am perfectly capable of cleaning up after myself," she said. "You need to get some rest. I am certain the pieces of this puzzle will start to fit together in the morning."

I gave her a look of surrender and made my way upstairs to my bedroom. Beau sat curled up barely visible on my pillow. I stripped out of my clothes and pulled on a pair of sweatpants and a loose t-shirt before climbing beneath the covers. I was careful to give the chameleon his space. I'd learned the hard way that his scales could be rather sharp when you landed on them wrong.

I nestled my head against the pillow and closed my eyes. I was just about to drift off when my phone rang with an incoming call. Groaning, I cracked one eye open to see Maggie's face flash on the screen. I pulled the phone towards me, setting it to speaker as I answered.

"How's Ryan?"

"I haven't been able to get in to see him. The police have him under a protective guard."

"Isn't that a good thing?" I couldn't hide the sleepiness in my voice.

"From what I could get out of the nurses it sounds like they are trying to pin things on him."

I sat bolt upright. "That's ridiculous. Ryan had no motive to hurt Lightspeed."

"No, but I'm guessing that Reese might have an in with the local law and they're more than willing to throw Ryan under the bus."

I was really beginning to dislike Ryan's father. "I'm sure Beau wouldn't mind helping you slip in without being seen."

"I have a nurse friend who owes me a favor. I promised I'd watch her cat when she goes out of town—and believe me it's definitely a sacrifice on my part—and she's going to see if she can get me in overnight tonight to see him."

"Not a cat person?"

"Severely allergic. But this is Vinnie. We do what we have to for our friends. I'll be fine."

"I love you."

"Did they have any idea why he ended up in a coma?"

"Not that I could get out of them. They were pretty busy when I got there. But like I said, I should be able to get in overnight and see him. With any luck, they've just sedated him, and I can lighten it. But we're going to need to find some evidence that proves Reese is behind this to keep Ryan out of jail."

We weren't just going to need that proof. We had to figure out what Drake was up to. I still didn't know whether Karl was reporting to him or Reese. For all I knew, he was playing both sides against each other. Maybe that was how we got them to admit the truth. I doubted Reese wanted to lose the track. If he found out that Drake had a history of tanking the businesses he swooped in to save, that might spark confrontation.

"I've been told by multiple people tonight that I need to get some sleep. So, I'm going to try to be a good girl and do that. Let me know what happens in the morning. Hopefully by then I'll have a plan on how to get Reese to confess and figure out exactly what Drake's game plan is."

"I love you, too, Darcy. Good night."

Setting the phone back on the nightstand, I snuggled beneath the blankets and shut my eyes.

SLEEP WAS NOT THE 'AHA MOMENT' I'd hoped for. I tossed and turned most of the night, seeing Light-speed's body collapsing onto the track over and over, with Ryan doing the same moments later. The clock read six o'clock when I finally gave up and got out of bed. Tania was still asleep—much to my surprise— when I made it downstairs. I stared at the lightening horizon in silence.

"Come on, Darcy. What are you missing?" I walked around the side of the kitchen table and pressed a finger to the tiny flowers starting to emerge in the planter.

"You didn't actually get to snoop yesterday," Sam's voice came from behind me. "That creeper stopped you in your tracks. But maybe it was for a reason?"

I turned to face the ghost. He'd abandoned his earlier green blazer for a more normal-looking dinner jacket in a deep purple. He'd donned matching eye shadow, too. "How so?"

"Well, you know that plants talk. Maybe they saw something? It's worth a shot is all I'm saying."

I had been feeling a bit cut off from my magic of late. Sure, I'd managed to uncover the hemlock in the hay, but it had felt very passive. Time to see if I could find a trail Drake wouldn't even know existed.

"It's worth a try," I agreed. "Fancy coming along to watch my back?'

He gave me a mischievous grin. "I thought you'd never ask."

"I have to admit, I never thought Deputy Ditzy would bring such drama to our little corner of the world," Sam said as I headed to High Time.

"Don't call him that. He's not ditzy," I scolded.

"I know he's not. It's just ... when he got to Brookhaven, he was a little green around the gills and the name just stuck. I'm dead, I'm allowed to be a stick-in-the-mud now and again."

"After everything he's gone through, he deserves our respect."

"I get it, I get it."

The parking lot was empty when we arrived. I

unlocked the employee entrance and made my way inside. I could see a light on in Sage's office and I stopped there first. The overhead had been left on and I could see the computer screen lit up with the screen saver. I didn't know her password. But luckily, when I jiggled the mouse, the screen popped up to reveal a blank internet browser set to a search page.

"What were you looking for Sage?"

No answer.

Not that I expected one.

Throwing caution to the wind, I typed Drake Gorman's name into the search and hit enter. A handful of results showed up detailing past business ventures he'd been involved in over the last few years, including a small article about his interest in the track. Nothing I didn't already know.

"Wait, what's that one down there?" Sam's translucent finger pointed to a result farther down the page.

I scrolled down to find a publicly available court filing related to one of his past businesses. It appeared to be criminal charges against the original owner of a chain of record shops for embezzling and money laundering. When I clicked on the page, I found a very brief mention of an unindicted co-conspirator, Drake Gorman.

"Oh, that's not good," I whispered.

"He's a very bad boy, isn't he?" The jovial lilt of Sam's voice was replaced by pure disdain.

"How much do you want to bet he sets these businesses up to take the fall for his illegal actions?"

"Definitely possible. But how would you even go about proving it?" Sam countered.

I didn't have that worked out yet. But there had to be a way. I still needed to find proof. If it was going to be anywhere, it would be back at the track. But first, I needed to see what I could find out about his mysterious guests the day before.

I cleared the search in the browser and retreated to the grow room. I did a quick survey of the room. Nothing was there that shouldn't have been. Still, I even got up on a chair and checked the light fixtures.

"What do you think they hid up there?" Sam called.

"Cameras? Listening devices? I don't know," I answered in a huff.

Satisfied Drake hadn't disrupted the sanctity of my space, I turned back to Sam. "Where did you see them interacting?"

Sam gestured to the space between the grow room and the break room. "Not sure how that's help-ful, though."

I waved him off as I lined myself up with that space. I took a few steps back, reaching out my hands to find the plants that were in the direct line of sight. Dipping my fingers into the soil, I got a good connection to the plants.

Let me see what you saw.

Much like the hay, the image was hazy at first before it resolved to show the room empty.

Sam disappeared first, replaced by a strange after-image of me talking to Drake. At least I knew I was in the right timeframe. I watched myself hurry away before Drake gave a small laugh and retrieved a phone from his pocket. "It's clear, come in the side."

My heart beat a little faster as I watched in horror as three men appeared. I tried to look at Drake's phone. Clearly, they'd waited long enough for me to leave the building. But I must have missed them by mere minutes. One of the men gestured to the other two silently and they scurried off. It wasn't until the man turned to address Drake that I realized it was Karl.

"You sure we should be setting up already, boss? That lady hasn't signed the paperwork yet."

"We need to be ready," Drake replied. "Things are getting too complicated at the track."

Karl waved his hand. "That will be fixed up in no time."

"And what if they decide Reese is at fault?"

"Well then we have some lovely evidence to support that theory, and you get to keep the rest of the business, boss. You are sitting pretty whether it's him or the kid taking the fall."

Drake rubbed his chin. "I knew I should have just bought them both out. But he was stubborn. And now I've got his bookies knocking down my doors looking for payments."

"I told you I took care of that. They know not to come looking to collect at the track."

"You better be right. We need to be back operating otherwise we're going to have problems of our own."

I let go of the plants and sucked in a breath. "Well, that explains who Karl is working for."

"Who's Karl again?" Sam prompted as I dusted the bits of soil from my fingers.

"The Head of Security at the track." Maybe Drake had brought Karl in—which seemed unlikely given that he hadn't been around long—or he'd managed to bribe him. Either way, there was clearly other activity going on at the track. It was time to try and put together a plan to get Drake and Reese to confront each other. But I had no idea how to go about it.

Leaving the shop behind, I made my way over to

Ginny's. I wasn't sure what I expected to find, but it wasn't Jayka sitting at the counter nursing one of Ginny's oversized mugs of coffee. The jockey eyed me warily as I sat beside her.

"I'm surprised you're still in town," I said. "I'd have thought you'd be heading off to another race."

"Like I said before, I don't live too far from the track. Honestly, I've been trying to work up the courage to go see Ryan in the hospital."

"I know he's in the ICU. A friend of mine wasn't even able to see him and she's a medical professional."

"I told you and your cop friend yesterday that Ryan found the results from the vet a week ago. Well, I didn't tell you that I told him he was probably just seeing things. Or that the vet sent him the wrong tests. But I went by yesterday and the vet admitted to me that he'd been using other horses' exams to cover Lightspeed for almost a year."

"Because Reese kept making bets on her and losing and he was trying to win it back?"

"That's what I assume."

"Do you think the vet would want to help take Reese down for the fraud?"

"Honestly? I don't know."

"Not to pile on, but I think Drake might be using

the track for dirty dealings, too. I found some articles and court filings that mentioned him as an unindicted co-conspirator in an embezzlement scam."

"Let me help make this right," Jayka said.

Now we just had to find a way to get two corrupt blokes together and make a full confession in front of law enforcement. Bugger.

13

Coming up with a plan was harder to do without caffeine. Luckily, Ginny materialized from the kitchen with a fresh pot and a mug as if she'd known I needed the boost. She eyed Jayka wordlessly as she handed me the mug filled almost to the brim.

"You're hatching one of your little plans to catch the bad guy. I can see it all over your face," Ginny noted with a hint of excitement in her tone.

That surprised me a little. She'd been fairly subdued since Halloween and the whole releasing her ancestral spirits on the town. But part of me couldn't be too annoyed at her. The incident had brought us closer. "I'm not really sure what we're going to do. But we have to try. Vinnie and his family are at stake."

That sobered Ginny's expression instantly. "I'd heard something about there being drama at the track a few towns over. I didn't realize it had anything to do with Vinnie."

"His cousin is the jockey who got hurt. His family owns the horse that died and the track—"

"And now because of me, some crook is using the place to do who knows what," Jayka interrupted.

"Something tells me there was nefarious dealings going on before Drake Gorman walked onto the scene," I pointed out.

"That Aussie guy trying to wine and dine Sage?" Ginny's tone carried a strong dose of disgust.

"Don't worry, I'm not going to let him ruin High Time's reputation or hurt Sage's business in any way," I promised.

"Well, something tells me you aren't going to get this done without Vinnie," Ginny noted. "He's no doubt invested in seeing his family protected."

"It's a little unsettling watching him push Maggie and I to, uh ... bend the rules."

"I'm sure he hasn't let you do anything that would interfere with prosecuting the case," Ginny noted.

I thought back to what Maggie and I had done. Technically, I hadn't had a reason to be at the track once the police released the scene. But I hadn't touched anything or left any prints behind. Vinnie had been careful not to contaminate the scene in Lightspeed's stall. And Maggie hadn't hacked Ryan's social media. And her getting into Vinnie's was barely a step over the line.

"We've tried to be discreet," I agreed. "But if I'm being honest, I'm feeling a little out of my depth here. Like ... I want to help Vinnie. He's my friend, but what can I really do?"

"He's at least trying to get justice," Jayka muttered.

"You can do plenty," Ginny answered.

Just then, my phone buzzed with an incoming text from Maggie.

> Things are still uncertain with Ryan.
> Did what I could, but I need to
> recharge.

"What does that mean, she did what she could?" Jayka looked at my phone screen before I could close out of the message app.

I swallowed the lump that had formed in my throat. I gave Ginny a plaintive look, hoping she'd help me explain that Maggie was a healer and was trying to bring Ryan out of the coma with magic. Ginny poured herself a cup of coffee and leaned on the edge of the counter on the server side.

"Do you believe in magic?" She arched a brow at the other woman and took a long sip from her mug.

"Seriously?"

"Oh, I wouldn't lie about something like that," Ginny answered.

"Not sure she could anyway," I added.

"Your friend is doing magic?"

"Girlfriend. She's a healer. We think someone might have done something to keep Ryan from speaking out. But she didn't seem to have much luck."

"Sorry, that's just a lot to process. Does Ryan know about it?'

"It's a family trait. Have you ever wondered why he's so good with the horses?"

Jayka let out a soft laugh. "Now that you mention it, yeah, he has always had a way with the animals. I thought he was just a decent and kind guy."

"He's an empath of sorts, but only with animals. When Lightspeed collapsed, he felt it. We think that's partly why he collapsed. But it also looked like he might have been poisoned, too."

"By whom?"

"I think it could have been Reese."

"His own father? God, that's ..." Her brow furrowed and she grew quiet. Ginny and I both leaned in, not wanting to miss her next statement. "I don't think it was Reese."

"Uh, I know it's going to sound kind of weird, but I've seen Reese literally feeding Lightspeed the poison," I said.

"No, I mean, that's awful but I don't think he'd hurt Ryan."

"How do you know?"

"I didn't think much of it, but right before the race I saw the security guy give Ryan a drink."

"Karl? Big guy, bald. Looks like he could crush you with one hand?"

"Yeah, that's the one."

"Do you know how long he's been working there?"

"At the track? A couple of years maybe."

Okay, that answered one question. Drake must have bought him off when he came into the picture.

Jayka rubbed her forehead. "But why would Karl want to hurt Ryan?"

"Because he's working for Drake. I bet whatever plan Reese came up with, Drake either is involved or knows about it and is going to hold it over his head as leverage."

"You've got to find a way to turn the two of them against each other," Ginny suggested.

"I can talk to the vet. I know he's got a guilty conscience right now after he came clean to me. I don't want to hurt him more, but he's complicit in this," Jayka said.

"What do these men all have in common? What's driving them?" Ginny pressed.

"Money," Jayka and I answered in unison.

Ginny smirked and gestured towards me with her coffee mug. "That's your angle. Use the promise or the threat of money to get them to reveal their hands."

"But we have to do it with the police present, so they see and hear it. They need to be taken down and the local cops, they're either the laziest people in the world, or they're just as corrupt as Drake and Reese," I pointed out.

"Good thing, Rick got in touch with the State Police, then." Vinnie stood in the doorway, looking rough around the edges. But I didn't spy any dark circles under his eyes. He crossed the threshold to reveal Rick standing behind him.

Rick sidled up to the counter and Ginny put

another cup of coffee down for him. "When I mentioned Drake Gorman's name, their ears perked right up."

"I found some court filings that mentioned Drake, linking him to fraud and embezzlement," I pointed out.

"Oh, he's wanted overseas for a lot more than that. He's been using the businesses he invests in to launder drug money," Rick replied. "And when I told the State Police, he was looking to do it to someone in my town ... well, they agreed to let us come in as back-up."

I knew the guy had rubbed me the wrong way. It also explained why he was so interested in the dispensary. What better way to launder money from illegal drugs than through a place that sells them legally. And if the other businesses he'd invested in had less than aboveboard things happening, he could slink away when the focus turned to them. It was a brilliant scheme; but one he wasn't going to get away with for much longer.

"So, we have to find a way to get Drake, Karl, and Reese in the same place and admit their parts of what's going on," I confirmed.

"The track makes the most sense for this to

happen," Vinnie said. "The evidence is probably still there, too."

"Hope you don't mind twisting the vet's arm to cooperate," I added. "Jayka thinks she can convince him to demand more money from Reese for his silence."

"Police use cooperating witnesses all the time to bring down bigger perpetrators," Rick replied.

"So, we just need to get the State Police on board with our little sting," I sighed. "They're probably not going to let any of us near this."

"That assumes they even know we're there," Vinnie replied.

Ginny fixed him with a disbelieving look. "Do not tell me you just suggested using magic to sneak into an active police operation, Vincent."

"Would it be less horrifying if I told you I already gave him my blessing?" Rick took a long sip from his coffee mug.

"I'd say who are you and what have you done with my brother? But, given recent events, maybe you're willing to be a little more lenient with stepping outside the bounds of the law."

"Vinnie's like family, Ginny. You know I won't stand for someone that going after my blood."

"Now that sounds like my brother."

"We're going to need to hurry. From what I heard, it sounds like Drake intends to have the track operational today. We don't want to make a huge scene in front of a big crowd," I interjected, trying to get the conversation back on track.

"Even if Reese did what you said to his own horse, there's no way he'd be willing to get the track up and running again the next day," Jayka argued.

"I tend to agree. If he did this for an insurance payout, he'd have to wait for the vet to sign off on the paperwork and the insurance company to review it. All of that could take a few days at least."

"Then I think it's time we let Reese know that he doesn't have as much time as he thought." I looked at Jayka. "Talk to the vet. Get him on board."

"I'll have Rick loop in the State Police. I'm sure they'd be happy to run this through proper channels and make it legit."

"That gets Reese in play, but what about Karl and Drake?"

"You get the vet to demand enough money that Reese has to go after whatever's at the track. How much you want to bet Drake's got some type of program on the computer that alerts him when money moves around?" Ginny chimed in.

"And if they try to run off with the money?" Jayka sounded nervous.

"Well, that's why the police will be there monitoring everything," I replied.

"You want to look these guys in the eye when they go down. You should be there, and you shouldn't have to hide." She pointed to me and gave me a once over. "You could be me."

"You can't be serious. That's never going to work. They've all met me and know I'm not you."

"Hang on ... it could work. At least with Reese," Vinnie said. "My uncle's never been great with faces." He eyed Jayka. "How often have you met or spoken with my uncle?"

"Not that often. Mostly I've interacted with Ryan."

"It could work."

I wasn't sure I liked the idea of putting myself in the middle of this without backup from people I trusted. And there was every chance that Karl and Drake recognized me and the whole thing blew up in our faces. "I'm not saying no, I just need to think about it for a minute."

"Think quick, Darcy. You're right. If Drake is opening up the track today, we've only got a few hours to get this done."

Vinnie stepped away, pulled out his phone,

dialed a number, and turned his back on us. I blocked out his voice as I tried to sort through my emotions. My stomach knotted from a healthy dose of fear. I normally didn't try to put myself in the middle of dangerous situations. Sure, sometimes I landed there, but it wasn't deliberate. This would be me purposely walking into a scenario that could turn very ugly. But Vinnie was my friend, and I was invested in seeing justice for Ryan and for Light-speed. And I owed it to Sage, to keep her from making a disastrous decision for the dispensary, too.

I wished I could talk to Maggie. I knew she'd steer my decision right. But she'd spent all night at the hospital trying to help Ryan. Still, I knew she wouldn't be happy if I did this without telling her first.

"I'll be right back."

I moved to the booth where I'd met Jayka the day before and opened my contacts list. I tapped Maggie's name near the top of the list and waited while the line rang. She answered on the third ring.

"Darcy? Everything okay?"

"You don't sound like you were asleep," I noted.

"I tried, but I think I have a way to get Ryan to wake up. I'm mixing up some things right now and then I'm going to head back to the hospital. That nurse friend of mine said she'd let me in one more time."

"I have no doubt you'll get him up and about in no time."

"Why do I get the sense you weren't calling just to check up on me?"

"Because I think we have a way to get Reese and Drake off the streets for good and atone for what they've done."

"Drake?"

There wasn't time to explain. "Just trust me, he's not a good person and he's putting a lot of people in danger."

"Please tell me the next words out of your mouth aren't 'including me.'"

"Vinnie thinks it's a good idea. And I wouldn't be alone. The State Police are involved, too."

"Darcy, that doesn't make it better. I don't want my girlfriend in the middle of some standoff with the police and bad guys. And in case you forgot, not everyone knows about or appreciates magic."

"I will be careful. But I think I need to do this ... for Ryan and for Vinnie. He asked for my help, and I can't say no." I stopped short of adding that if something did go wrong, I always had her healing abilities to fall back on.

"I'm not going to talk you out of it. Just ... if things feel off, get out of there."

"I promise I won't take any unnecessary risks."

"I love you."

"I love you, too."

I ended the call, took a deep breath, and returned to the counter. Vinnie appeared to have finished his call, too.

"The State Police are willing to support us. Apparently, the vet was already on their radar. They've brought him in for questioning and are floating the idea of cooperating. We just need to wait for their go-ahead that things are moving forward."

"We can't wait for the red tape. We need to be there at the track, ready to make a move," I protested.

"I agree with you. That's why we're going to head over there now."

"I'm coming, too. You're going to need to look the part. Besides, I think I have a way to get Drake there, even if Reese doesn't fall for the bribe," Jayka announced. "He slid into my DMs looking for something I wasn't going to give him. But people change their minds. Maybe I'm more open to hearing what he has to say?"

"You're putting a lot on the line for someone who's not even that good of a friend," I pointed out.

"Yeah, well, Ryan is a decent guy. And the more I think about it the more I'm trying to make up for putting us all in this situation in the first place. I should have just ignored the guy. But initially, Drake was charming. We talked about racing and riding in general. I really thought he was the answer to helping Reese get out of his gambling spiral."

Time to set things right.

14

My nerves were taut as we crammed into the back of Brookhaven's police cruiser. It would look conspicuous to show up to a takedown in a marked vehicle, but I didn't say anything to Vinnie as he drove with Rick in the front passenger seat. Even though the State Police knew we were supposed to be there, I'd swung by the B&B first and enlisted Beau's help. Even if he wasn't helping me sneak around, he could be very useful. I'd earned a curious look from Jayka when I'd settled in with Beau perched on my shoulder. Thankfully, she'd rolled with the 'magic chameleon' explanation.

Beside me, Jayka was busy tapping away on her phone. I tried to peer over and see what she was sending to entice Drake to meet her at the track, but she had one of those screen protectors that obscured spying.

"I know it's not my fault, but I can't help feeling like I brought this on," I blurted as Vinnie signaled to get into the lane that would take us to the exit off the highway.

"Darcy, you didn't do any of this. It's pretty clear Reese has been planning this for a long time. None of this is on you. But I am grateful you're helping me put things right. Without you and Maggie, I'm not sure anyone would have bothered to look into it."

I should have asked Maggie to check with her nurse friend to see if anyone matching Karl's description had stopped by before Ryan had fallen into the coma. But there wasn't time now. The track loomed ahead of us and Vinnie slowed the car, pulling into a spot as far from the front entrance as he could manage. I spotted another car in the lot a few spaces over. Two people were seated inside. The passenger side door opened and a slender woman with short-cropped red hair climbed out. She approached our cruiser and Vinnie rolled down the window.

"You the guys from Brookhaven?"

"Yes, Ma'am. We have some people we've got in play," Vinnie replied. He pointed at Jayka and I.

The woman leaned over and studied us with a curious expression before turning her attention back to Vinnie. "We've got surveillance set up, but no one's come in or out in a few hours."

"We're working on that," Rick interceded. "You have the vet, I take it."

The redhead waved to the other vehicle and the driver side rear door opened and the man I'd seen on the surveillance video appeared. He looked sweaty even from this distance and his shirt was untucked and rumpled. He was clearly feeling the weight of what he'd done.

Good.

"Our friend Brian here has sent the owner a text suggesting that the price of his silence has gone up."

"You're sure that this is going to be enough to get me out of this?" His voice was high and squeaky.

The redhead let out a laugh. "You get Reese to transfer the money, and we'll make sure the judge knows you cooperated."

"Why help Reese at all? You had to know what he was doing wasn't right?" I leaned forward to address the man.

"It wasn't that big a deal at first. I certified Light-speed to race when she was coming off an injury. But

I always made sure she had enough meds to get her through without being in pain."

"What you did to that horse is unethical," Jayka spat. "You're the reason she's dead now. She should have been retired and cared for."

"I didn't tell him to do anything."

"But you went along with his scheme, because he lined your pockets," I retorted.

"And you doctored the results using other people's horses. You could have cost those people their careers," Jayka added angrily.

Before either of us could say more, Brian pulled a phone from his front pants pocket. He passed it to the redhead who in turn showed it to Vinnie. "Looks like we're on for the exchange."

Vinnie squinted at the phone. "You really sure he's going to show up for that amount of money?"

I craned my neck to see that Brian was asking for $10,000. That certainly looked like a lot of money. But it occurred to me that I had no idea how much Reese had been paying the vet to keep quiet and doctor the test results.

"He's probably got at least five times that on the premises," Vinnie noted. "I mean, at least back when I was younger the track turned a decent profit."

"That's not a bad idea," the redhead said. "Get him to give you everything he's got."

Brian blanched. "I—I can't do that."

"Sure, you can." I climbed out of the back of the cruiser and rounded the car. Beau settled along my right shoulder, draping his tail down my back. "You're trying to atone for what you did. If that means asking him for everything he's got, you do it. And you're not going to be alone. I'll be there, too."

His brow scrunched up. "What do you mean?"

"Guess I'll be undercover with you."

"Well, whatever you're going to do, you better get moving. He says he's twenty minutes out," the redhead said.

Jayka climbed out next and produced a silver key. "Come on, I've got my riding gear in my locker. If we're lucky it will fit you well enough to convince him you're me."

'Useful elsewhere'

Beau's voice echoed in my head, and I watched as he inclined his head towards Vinnie, who still sat in the driver seat of the cruiser. For a moment, I didn't understand what he meant.

'Watch his back.'

"You sure, mate? That'd be giving up our little secret," I whispered to the chameleon.

'Worth the risk'

I rounded the front of the car and bent down to the open window. "I think he might be able to help you find the evidence you need to nail Karl for blackmail and covering things up."

Vinnie's face shifted to a look of surprise as Beau detached himself from my shoulder and settled on Vinnie's arm, blending into the fabric.

"Fair warning, it's going to feel a bit strange when he gives you the edge."

"What ... edge?"

I waved my fingers in what I hoped was a 'magical illusion' pantomime. Vinnie just undid his seatbelt and climbed out of the car. Rick followed suit, clearly letting Vinnie take the lead on this whole operation.

"So that's how you get around unnoticed," Vinnie said with a wink.

"Shhh."

He mimed zipping his lips.

"Oh, and you're going to want to check the security hub's computer," I offered before Jayka grabbed me by the arm and led me away from the parking lot.

"So, what did you tell Drake to get him to come down here?" I watched Jayka tap a keypad by a large exterior metal door, similar to the one we'd gone through to access the stables. It opened with an electronic beep and a tiny red light flipped to green.

"I said I'd had a change of heart after things went down with Ryan and I was interested in hearing what he had to offer me."

The door opened into a short corridor. I could pick up on the scent of straw and horse feed. I spotted a small window that looked into the stables off to our right. Jayka motioned for me to follow her the opposite way and after a few paces I found myself in a cramped locker room with two long benches taking up most of the space between the two rows of lockers.

"Not exactly accommodating in here," I noted.

"It's not like we're in here long." Jayka pulled open one of the lockers at the far end and began pulling out riding pants and a jacket.

"You said Karl gave Ryan something to drink before the race started. Where'd you see him do it?"

Jayka gestured to the other end of the locker room next to a tall trash can. "Right there."

"Did Ryan drink all of it?"

"Honestly, not sure. He could have taken a couple of sips and tossed it. To be polite, you know?"

As Jayka finished pulling gear out of her locker, I

bent over the trash can and carefully nudged the lid aside. Clearly, in all of the haste to deal with Lightspeed's death, no one had come through to collect the rubbish from the bin. A travel cup with a cardboard holder sat on top of the pile.

"Do you have a glove?" I held out my hand behind me as I spoke.

"Uh, sure. Why?"

I made a grabbing motion and waited for her to hand me a glove. It had thick leather and didn't quite fit my hand as I pulled it on. But at least I wasn't going to contaminate the scene more. I picked up the cup from the trash and shook it lightly. The contents sloshed around. I opened it and took a whiff. My vision blurred, and I could feel the wooziness of the hemlock exposure from the day before coming on. The drink had to be why Ryan had hemlock in his bloodstream.

Setting it back in the trash where I'd found it, I tugged the glove off and retrieved my phone, firing off a text to Vinnie.

> Check the locker room too. Possible Ryan was drugged before the race. Cup in the trash.

Setting my phone on one of the benches, I took

my jacket off and turned to face Jayka. "I really hope lying to Reese and making him think you want in on the blackmail money doesn't ruin things with Ryan."

"I got people involved in his life, because I was trying to help. This actually does some good. I'm sure he'll understand."

I pulled on her riding jacket and pants. They weren't a perfect fit, but we only needed to keep up the ruse long enough for the State Police to get the evidence they needed—Reese attempting to pay off Brian.

"Do you do this sort of thing often? Putting yourself in harm's way for strangers?"

"Uh, not intentionally. But I do seem to have a habit of ending up in the middle of things."

"You could just walk away."

I gave her a pointed look. "So could you."

"Fair point."

Just then, Jayka's phone pinged with an incoming message. Her cheeks flushed. "He says he'll be here in ten minutes."

"Right on time, then."

I watched Jayka tug down her shirt and loosen her hair, so it flowed down over her right shoulder in an alluring manner. She was putting all of her charms on full display.

"Try to keep him occupied long enough for Vinnie and the State Police to get the evidence they need from Reese."

"I'll do my best," she promised and pointed me back towards the door. "Hang a left and follow the corridor all the way down. You'll find a little alcove that leads you out under the stairs by the track.

I was two steps out the door when she tossed me a riding helmet. "Just in case, this could help disguise you."

My palms grew sweaty as I followed the route she'd laid out, taking me closer to the heart of danger. This was not at all how I'd envisioned the weekend turning out. I'd just wanted a nice trip with Vinnie and Maggie. Something simple and fun, not full of death and intrigue.

Focus, Darcy.

When I finally stepped out of the alcove beneath the stairs, I could hear the sound of low voices, and one sounded like the redhead officer. I emerged from the stairs and spotted Brian staring at his phone, shifting his weight from foot to foot, a clear sign of anxiety. The redhead spotted me, made a gesture that she was watching and disappeared from sight.

"I don't even know why he'd agree to give me

more money," Brian whined, starting to wring his hands.

"Because I found out what you were doing and you need money to stop me from going public with the scandal," I offered simply. "Clearly Reese is desperate, and we have to hope that he'll assume whatever payout he gets from the insurance company will cover whatever he pays you."

"You have an awful lot of faith in a man who purposely hurt his own horse."

"I have faith in the fact that justice will be served and that you're trying to pay penance for your part in it."

"I swear I didn't know he was drugging her or poisoning her. I was just giving her some steroids and pain meds to run on injured legs. That sort of thing."

"That doesn't make it better."

The squeal of tires on pavement cut the conversation short. I urged Brian to head out onto the track. It was better to do the exchange in an open space where there were more ways the police could see us and intervene if something went wrong. Heavy footsteps thudded on the concrete surface leading into the track proper and after a moment, Reese appeared. He had a case in one hand.

"You have some nerve," he snarled when he spotted Brian standing there.

I took a few steps off to the side. We had to draw this out as much as we could. We just needed time for Drake and hopefully Karl to show up. Brian fiddled with his shirt, and I realized too late that he'd been wired up by the State Police. They weren't leaving anything up to chance. My mouth went dry as fear crept in. Would Reese realize what was happening and back out of the deal?

"Did you bring it?" Brian's voice was an anxious falsetto as Reese approached him.

Reese thrust the case at Brian. "Of course I did. Take your money and get the hell off my damn track."

"Somewhere to be?" The question surprised Brian as much as it did me.

Reese rolled his eyes. "In case you didn't notice, my kid's in the hospital in a coma."

"I didn't know that." Brian glanced in my direction, and I mouthed the words 'more money' to him. "But you can't go yet."

Reese closed the distance between them and jabbed his finger in the vet's face. "And why not?"

"Because you've got more mouths to keep shut than you thought," I called, hoping I sounded braver than I felt in this moment. "I know what he's been doing for you. He used my horse to cover up bad results for you."

"You idiot. You had to go blabbing about what you did?" Reese spat in Brian's face.

"He didn't say anything. I figured it out on my own. And I'd be happy to go to the press and the police ..." I took a pause, long enough to draw Reese's attention. "Or you make it worth my while to stay quiet about everything and forget it even happened."

Reese backed up a step and rubbed his forehead. "How ... how much?"

Vinnie had suggested Reese had at least $50,000 at the track. That would certainly get his attention and Drake's too. "I want five times whatever you paid him."

Reese's cheeks blanched. "I don't have that kind of money on me right now."

"Ryan said you run a pretty profitable business here."

"Okay, okay. I don't have it in cash, but ... I can transfer it to you."

"What the hell did you say you were about to do with my money?" Reese spun to find Drake standing there, holding a gun aimed at his head.

15

$\mathcal{J}$ayka was nowhere in sight and that worried me. Not as much as the gun being pointed at Reese's head, though. I glanced around the track, praying the police would swoop in at the sight of the weapon. But nothing happened. Were they that intent on catching Drake that they would risk civilians? Surely, Rick wouldn't let that stand. Except, he wasn't in charge here. The State Police had no loyalty to me, and they were willing to risk Brian to make their case, too.

"W-what are you doing here?" Reese stammered, his gaze zeroed in on the gun.

"Not your concern. What is that I heard? You're willing to pay some girl you don't even know thousands of dollars of my money."

"You're co-owner. It's my money, too," Reese protested, his voice growing stronger.

"I knew I should have just gotten rid of you when I bought out your weak-willed brother. You've been more trouble than you're worth."

"Why keep him around then?" My words came out before I thought better of it. "Wouldn't it be easier to have no one else to answer to? Surely, you've learned from your past mistakes."

Drake's full attention was on me now. The gun muzzle swiveled, so it was directed my way now. "Wait, I know that voice."

I did my best not to panic. We'd only had two interactions. Surely, he couldn't remember me that vividly. He gestured to Reese. "Take off her helmet."

"Are you insane?" Reese protested.

Drake shifted the angle of the gun and fired off a shot, sending it pinging into the dirt at our feet. It took every ounce of my self-control not to jump back and let out an undignified yelp.

"I'll do it," Brian said. He moved to block Drake's view of me. Not the move I would have made with the man waving a loaded weapon around. "What are we supposed to do now? Why aren't they coming in?"

"I don't know. But we're going to be fine."

I unclipped the strap of the helmet and pulled it off, so it no longer obscured my face. I took the few seconds it took Brian to move back to facing Drake to survey our surroundings. The track was fake turf mostly with actual dirt around the edges. I couldn't see anything living, but there had to be something. I focused my attention inward, calling on my magic. I needed it now more than ever to be easy and effortless.

The fear coursing through my veins made it harder to access. It sputtered in my mind's eye before I got ahold of it and let it blossom and grow within me.

If you're out there, help me.

My vision grew hazy around the edges. I could see something beyond the entrance to the track—shrubs of some kind. They were just beginning to regain their greenery after winter. I could also see the police starting to make a move towards the front door. At least we wouldn't be alone for long. Not that I wanted to be performing blatant acts of magic in front of an audience. Still, I had a feeling Drake wasn't going to leave me much choice in that matter.

"You're the plant girl from the dispensary!" Drake howled, his gun moving back to me, and leveling at my chest.

Reese studied me. "Wait a minute ... that's right. You were here with my nephew." He made a grab for the case he'd given to Brian. "You're working with the police!"

"No, I'm not!" Brian yelped, scampering out of range, his hands firmly clamped on the case's handle.

"You brought the police to my door?" Drake growled, turning his attention back to Reese. "I knew it was a fool's errand to get in bed with a degenerate gambler. You couldn't even keep your own bookies happy."

"I made this place a lot of money. I made you money."

"Oh, please. You were on the verge of collapse when I came in. Your brother knew it and had the sense to get out. I'm the reason you're still afloat."

There was every chance they'd get each other to incriminate themselves in their separate schemes, but it could take ages. We needed to diffuse the situation. Or at least speed up the inevitable.

"Didn't you wonder why things were booming all of a sudden? Surely you had to know that the audience wasn't any bigger." I addressed Reese. "Or were you too busy making sure you could keep betting on your own horse?"

"People were betting more," Reese said defensively.

"How'd you figure it out, little miss plant lover?" Drake snapped, taking a step closer to me.

"It wasn't hard. I got a bad vibe from you when you toured the dispensary. I knew something was off when you were there and no one else was. And doing a simple internet search brought up your past criminal involvement."

"What involvement?" Reese cast a wary look between Drake and me.

"Oh, he's got a habit of investing in businesses and then making them tank. Not before they see a big surge though. I'm guessing he needs the cover for the dirty tricks he's playing. What was it ... laundering money?"

Reese glowered at Drake. "You used my legitimate business to move dirty money?"

Drake let out a laugh. "Think you've got it all figured out, do you? What proof have you got?"

"Oh, nothing really. Except how much do you want to bet on Karl being loyal? I mean you bought his allegiance when you came in. I'm sure if the police offered him something lucrative enough, he'd tell them where all the bodies are buried."

"Maybe I should go to the police, offer them a

look at the books. Put you away for good?" Reese shouted.

"Oh please. You wouldn't dare risk that. Not with your little habit. Oh, I know all about what you've been paying the good horse doctor for. Hiding the truth about your sick old horse. God, you thought you were being clever, didn't you?"

Reese's face deepened to a shade of red I'd never seen before. "You're lying."

Drake waved the gun about. "You forgot about all the cameras? They're everywhere. You can't hide anything from me. I know all about you dosing the horse. You thought you'd get away with it and what, get a payout from the insurance company?"

I had to admit, Drake was doing a pretty good job of getting Reese to confess to the fraud. I had to assume that Brian's mic and camera were capturing it all for the eventual trial. Drake began to pace in front of us, the gun shifting its target as he went.

I could still feel my power just below the surface. I had confidence in my abilities now. I knew that whatever I asked the surrounding plants to do, they'd obey. But that meant knowing what I needed them to do. Just as I was about to wing it, Brian threw the case up in the air and made a run for it.

"I can't do this!" he shouted, beating a hasty retreat.

The case landed on the ground, hitting the clasp keeping it shut as it did so. The lid popped open and neat stacks of hundred-dollar bills spilled out. The wind picked up, starting to carry them off. Drake and Reese each lunged forward, trying to catch the errant bills.

"You know he got Karl to poison Ryan," I blurted, trying to redirect their attention.

Reese stopped clamoring for the money and stared at me. "What are you talking about?"

"Ryan didn't collapse after Lightspeed went down, because she fell on him. He was poisoned. I'm guessing you weren't very careful with how and where you stored the hemlock. That's what you used to make Lightspeed sick, right?'

"How could you possibly know that?'

"I know my plants. He got to Ryan. Maybe to send you a message, I don't know. But I bet you that Ryan's coma is Karl's doing, too."

Reese's gaze went unfocused for a moment. "I thought he was there, because he wanted to support Ryan."

"Don't act like the caring paternal figure now.

Everyone knows you couldn't stand your kid," Drake drawled.

"He and I didn't get along all the time, but that didn't mean I wanted to hurt him."

"But you were hurting him," I pointed out. "You didn't think what he could do was manly enough. But that didn't mean you didn't believe in his gift. You knew that every time you made Lightspeed race while injured or put her in distress when you fed her tainted feed that Ryan could sense something was wrong. Maybe he would have collapsed from the weight of her pain. And that would have been your fault."

Reese rounded on Drake, bending down as he did so to scoop up the case. He secured it shut before swinging it up towards the other man's head. It connected with the side of Drake's face, leaving a bloody gash in its wake. Drake snatched the case from Reese's hand, returning the gesture. Reese stumbled back and wheezed as he tried to catch his breath. Only Drake leveled the gun at Reese.

Time to bring a little magic to the scene. I curled my fingers at my sides and envisioned the shrubs out front reaching down along the ground, snaking their roots through the front gates and slithering to wrap around Drake and hold him immobile. Maybe then the police would descend and put an end to this.

"I could just end it right now. Not the first time I've had to clean up a mess like this," Drake admitted. He pulled back the hammer on the gun and stepped closer to Reese.

"I wouldn't risk it. All those cameras," I reminded him. The roots and branches of the shrubs appeared behind me, slowly rising to Drake's full height.

"And you forget, I have the head of security on my payroll," Drake snarled.

"Could he erase the feed before the police get here?" I retorted.

"If there were police, they'd have been here already," Drake scoffed.

I hated to admit he had a point. There was no reason to hold back now. "You're not going anywhere."

I waved my hands in a winding gesture as I pictured the branches wrapping around him. At the last second, Reese lunged forward, making a mad grab for the gun. Instinctively, I hit the ground, covering my head with my arms. A shot rang out and I forced myself to look up. Drake stood trapped in the branches I'd summoned. Reese slumped against the roots that were keeping Drake's legs immobile. The gun sat on the ground a foot away from Reese. He was dazed as a small, neat hole had pierced his left arm.

"Darcy!" Vinnie's voice boomed from off to my left.

I looked up, but saw nothing except a strange ripple in the air. Like a heat mirage was moving through the space. *Beau.* I'd nearly forgotten that he'd gone with Vinnie to have his back. Slowly, I stood up and brushed dirt from the front of Jayka's borrowed riding pants.

"Took you long enough."

"Get this bloody thing off me!" Drake howled, clawing futilely at the branches. They appeared to tighten of their own accord, drawing tiny pinpricks of blood from his forearms.

"I told you, you weren't going anywhere," I repeated. Drake struggled some more and this time, I intentionally urged the branches to clamp down on his upper arms. They drew more blood. "Oh, and that's for trying to drag Sage into your criminal scheming."

"He—he ... shot me," Reese whimpered. "That ... that wasn't supposed to happen. I saw ... "

"Stop lying, Uncle Reese," Vinnie said, hauling the man to his feet. Rick approached through the stands, gun held aloft and ready. Vinnie locked eyes with the police chief before turning back to his uncle. "And you won't get sympathy from me." Without warning, Vinnie leaned back and took a solid slug at his uncle's face. His knuckles connected with the man's jaw.

"Guess you didn't see that coming," Vinnie muttered.

"He hit me!" Reese protested, trying futilely to rub his jaw.

"I didn't see anything," Rick said coolly. "Did you, Darcy?"

His intense amber gaze told me the correct answer. "No, Sir, nothing."

Reese let out a pained hiss as the redheaded police officer finally materialized with her partner in tow, their weapons drawn. The redhead eyed Drake's unconventional bindings, but said nothing as they took Reese into custody, slapping handcuffs on his wrists.

"You are under arrest for bribery, extortion, and insurance fraud. And that's just the tip of the iceberg." The female officer led Reese away as she continued to recite his rights. He shot his nephew a pleading look, but Vinnie turned his back, making it clear where he stood.

"You left your phone in the locker room," Vinnie began, looking at me. "Maggie texted. The potion she tried was able to wake Ryan from the coma. They're giving him some extra meds to make sure the hemlock cleared his system completely. He's going to be okay," Vinnie told me, handing over the phone.

"I'm glad he's going to be alright. What happened to Jayka?"

"Turned out it was Karl who messaged her from Drake's account. He's in custody, too. And she's fine. Well, a little pissed off, but fine. Oh, and when we confronted Karl with the evidence he left behind in the locker room, he flipped on Drake in a heartbeat. We've got enough to take them all down and put them away for a very long time."

"Come on, we should get that hand looked at. Maybe Maggie can fix you up."

He flexed his fingers, the abrasions turning red and angry. "I'll be fine."

"Don't be a hero, Vinnie. Let her patch you up."

"I guess it can't hurt." He sounded almost disappointed.

"Come on, we stopped a notorious drug dealer and money launderer, and we uncovered an insurance scheme. You have to be happy about that."

"I just wish it hadn't come at the expense of my family."

"Look at it this way, it brought you back to the people who matter. Blood doesn't always mean they're the people you count on."

"You do know how to look on the bright side, don't you?"

"Believe me, it's not always easy."

"Uh, how exactly am I supposed to take him into custody?" the redhead's partner asked, pointing at Drake.

Vinnie and I exchanged a look. I laughed, waving my hands again. I encouraged the branches and roots to recede enough for the officer to get handcuffs on Drake's wrists.

"Now I have to explain weird magic plants," he muttered to himself.

"Trust me, you get used to it," Vinnie called.

The officer managed to free Drake the rest of the way and dragged him out of sight. That left Vinnie and I standing in the heart of the track. What had started out as a trip to relax and try something new had ended up once again being more than either of us intended.

"Let's get out of here. I don't know about you, but I'm ready for a break from my weekend," Vinnie said with a soft laugh.

"Me, too. Let's go home."

16

The air was unseasonably warm as I stood outside of Maggie's building, two to-go cups from Ginny's in hand. I'd donned a thicker jacket and was regretting my decision when the door opened, and Maggie walked out. She accepted the cup of coffee I offered and took a long pull.

"I just can't stop thinking about Vinnie and Ryan," I said as we walked side by side in the direction of the station. Vinnie had insisted we were there when Ryan was released from the hospital.

"Family is complicated. We both know that. But they are resilient guys. I have to believe that they'll bounce back from this. Besides, they're back in each other's lives and that has to be a good thing."

"I just wish it didn't involve so much heartache and loss," I sighed and looped one arm through hers.

"I know."

We passed by Ginny's café, and I spotted the lit-up sign for High Time. I hadn't had a chance to check in with Sage since everything happened with Drake and Reese. Though I'd hoped she'd heard enough to back out of any deal she'd been considering. Given that Drake had used the track to launder money, I had no doubt he'd intended to do the same with any franchise Sage granted him.

In short order, we reached the station, and the automatic doors slid apart to reveal Chief Hayes standing there. Was he expecting us? That set my nerves on edge. He'd been largely absent from this investigation—as one would expect when it fell outside his jurisdiction—but he looked all business now. He caught me looking at him and his shoulders slackened a little.

"Vinnie asked me to give you a ride to the hospital," he explained before either Maggie, or I could question him.

"He does know we're capable of going there on our own, right?" I pointed out.

The chief shrugged. "He won't say it, but I think

he hopes having a police presence will make his cousin feel more at ease."

I wasn't going to begrudge Vinnie wanting to make Ryan feel more comfortable. And maybe it would deter some of Drake's thugs from taking action against Ryan in the wake of their boss' arrest. So, Maggie and I dutifully followed the chief around the back of the station. I expected him to lead us to his cruiser. Instead, he unlocked a sleek sports car.

"I think they're both compensating for something," I whispered in Maggie's ear as we climbed into the backseat.

"This, if you must know, was a gift from Ginny," the chief proffered unsolicited.

"It's lovely," I noted in sheepish embarrassment.

He flashed me a small smirk before climbing behind the wheel and revving the engine. Without further delay, he pulled out onto the street, and we were off. For such a fancy car, the engine was surprisingly quiet as we zipped along the highway. I couldn't be sure that the chief wasn't trying to show off and I smiled in spite of myself as the hospital came into view.

He pulled the car into a spot in the visitor lot and climbed out, adjusting his holster, and donning his hat. In the early morning sunlight, the amber flecks in his otherwise brown eyes glinted vibrantly. For a split second, I recalled the way his body had transformed from man to large mountain cat and back again. Brookhaven really was full of magical marvels. Squaring his shoulders, Rick led the way into the lobby.

Finding Ryan's room wasn't difficult and one of the on-call nurses even offered Maggie and I a wave of recognition as we walked by. I caught the sound of laughing coming from Ryan's room and picked up my pace, pushing past Chief Hayes through the door. Vinnie's cousin sat on the edge of the bed looking almost back to normal. I could still see the hints of the ordeal in the sunken skin around his eyes and the way his cheeks were still a bit more flushed than was healthy. But he was out of the hospital gown and dressed in a clean t-shirt and jeans and moving under his own power. Vinnie stood by the window, studying something in the distance.

"You didn't have to bring the cavalry to walk me out of here," Ryan announced when he spotted us.

"You're my family, Ry," Vinnie replied, clapping him on the shoulder before nodding towards Maggie, the chief, and me. "And so are they. It didn't seem right not to have them here."

"I really appreciate everything you two did to help find out what happened to Lightspeed."

"You don't have to thank us. We're just glad we could be there for you," Maggie replied, placing a hand on his forearm. "And we are so very sorry for your loss."

"I knew my dad was doing shady things. I felt something was off when he cut Vinnie's dad out of the business and brought in Gorman. I just wish I'd said something. Or pushed back when he insisted on racing Lightspeed when I knew she was too old."

"Standing up to our parents is hard," Chief Hayes said.

"At least it sounds like Uncle Reese has pleaded guilty and is going to testify against Gorman," Vinnie interjected. "That should save Ryan from having to testify at all."

"I'll do whatever they need me to do," Ryan insisted.

"Resting up is the most important thing right now," Vinnie replied. 'Besides, trials take time."

"Vinnie's trying to convince me to come convalesce in Brookhaven," Ryan said, clearly changing the subject.

"Well, I know a good room for rent. Might even

convince the proprietor to give you the friends and family discount," I said with a laugh.

"I keep telling him that I'll be okay," Ryan insisted. "I'm not so fragile I can't go home to heal."

"It might not be about your healing," Maggie offered quietly and nodded towards Vinnie. "Just keep that in mind."

Ryan's cheeks burned a little brighter. "Uh, I should have thought about that."

A nurse with a dark brown bob stopped in, cutting the conversation short as she handed Ryan a pile of paperwork. Maggie and I stepped into the corridor to let the nurse review Ryan's discharge information with him. Maggie slid her hand into mine and gave it a squeeze.

"You were really brave the other day," Maggie said and rested her head on my shoulder.

"And here I thought you were going to tell me I was being reckless. Getting in between a money launderer and a grifter."

"Well, I mean, yes, I'd prefer my girlfriend take her personal safety seriously. But you are always going to step in to stop the bad guy when you can, because that's just who you are."

"Well, getting Ryan to the point where he can be

released from the hospital comes down to you. You figured out the poisoning and reversed it in time."

"The hospital would have gotten there eventually."

"But not without lasting damage. You are the real hero, Maggie."

"You two can come back in now," Ryan called, flagging us down.

Maggie straightened and led me into the room. Vinnie helped him with a light windbreaker and slid the stack of papers into a plastic bag from the hospital gift shop before Ryan took a step towards the door.

"You know, Vinnie has been telling me all about the cafe in town. I think I could use a good meal," Ryan proclaimed when we reached the lobby.

"Did he tell you about its owner and her propensity to get you to spill all of your secrets?" Chief Hayes asked with an uncharacteristic smile.

"Only that she's a real treasure," Ryan answered.

Chief Hayes fixed Vinnie with a quizzical look that seemed to carry a hint of warning before we headed for the parking lot. Did Vinnie have some sort of crush on Ginny? I followed the chief back to his sports car, only to realize that Vinnie had ridden his motorcycle here. That meant Ryan would be coming with us. Since there was no way that the hospital would let him get on the back of a motorcycle.

"Meet you at Ginny's," Vinnie called as he donned his helmet and a pair of aviator sunglasses.

Ryan settled into the passenger seat once Maggie and I had climbed in the back. Chief Hayes revved the engine again. Part of me wondered if it was some strange cultural thing I didn't understand, that if you had a fancy car, you had to let everyone know. Or if it was just a male thing.

"So, Ryan, what are you going to do now?" I asked as the car slid into the flow of traffic on the highway.

"He's just gotten out of the hospital, Darcy. Give the man a minute to breathe," Maggie chided.

"Honestly, I'm not entirely sure. I know I can't abandon the other horses that my dad was stabling and racing. I have to figure out if he was dosing just Lightspeed or if he was trying to hurt any of the others, too."

"I'd get a different vet," I offered.

He tried to turn around in the front seat, but the seatbelt kept him facing forward. "What do you mean?"

Apparently, Vinnie hadn't told him that the vet had been involved in covering up Reese's scheme. Not that he wouldn't have figured it out eventually.

"Brian, the vet, was being paid off to fake results to keep Lightspeed racing. Your father blackmailed him and tried to extort him to keep on top of his gambling debts.

"All this time, I thought he was making money off his bets because of his powers. I guess even a clairvoyant's luck runs out," Ryan said quietly.

Ryan grew silent as the trees on either side of the highway gave way to the familiar terrain just outside Brookhaven. The car passed Tyson's shop at the very edge of town and before long, we were back in the normal hustle and bustle of Brookhaven. Vinnie's motorcycle sat parked outside the cafe when we arrived. I even spotted Ginny inside, perched in her usual spot at the center counter. Vinnie waved us in from the front window, directing us to a booth at the very front of the establishment.

Ryan led the way inside, fixing Ginny with a polite, if flirty smile as he passed. Ginny arched a brow at her brother as he settled at the counter beside her. "Your escort duty over?"

"We'll see," the chief answered.

I was about to go join Vinnie and Ryan in the booth when Sage caught my arm and pulled me over to the far end of the counter. I had missed seeing her with Ginny pulling my focus. Before I could even ask what Sage needed, she pulled me into a fierce hug.

"Thank you."

"Oh, I didn't do anything really."

"I knew something felt off about the whole offer. I just read that Drake's been arrested for money laundering and being in league with some guy running illegal gambling."

"I wanted to tell you what I'd found out about him, but it wasn't my place."

She patted her bag where a stack of papers protruded. Printouts of the information Maggie and I had found about Drake during our search for the truth. The same papers I'd asked Tania to slip to Sage anonymously.

"Something tells me you did warn me as soon as you could."

"I'm just glad it all worked out and no one else got hurt or pulled into something they couldn't get out of."

"We really are lucky to have you around, Darcy."

I brushed off the compliment. "Really, I didn't do anything. I was in the right place at the right time; and I didn't do any of it alone. I had loads of help."

"Since you came to town, things have definitely not been boring. And maybe that's the point," Sage mused. "I'm just trying to say I'm grateful that you came here, is all."

"Well, I appreciate you taking a chance on me all those months ago. You changed my life, too."

I gave my boss a quick hug before leaving her at the counter. I gave Ginny and Chief Hayes a quick nod as I went to join Maggie, Vinnie, and Ryan. They'd already ordered as the server brought over several plates with sandwiches and burgers.

"I hope you don't mind, I ordered for you," Maggie said.

"You know me too well." I leaned in and kissed her.

"Ryan was just telling us he's thinking of keeping the track going," Vinnie said. "Not what I would have chosen personally, but then again it isn't my decision."

Ryan nudged Vinnie in the ribs. "You could always get back in."

Vinnie shook his head. "I'll take having you back in my life, Ry. I don't need to get mired in all that drama and trauma. And you really shouldn't either."

"I want to run it differently. Have the track work as a collective with some of the other jockeys. And I was thinking, we could make it more like a training ground for new riders and maybe even vet tech students. I want the track to do some good."

"I think that sounds like an amazing way to change something that hurt so many people and give back to the community," I said.

"I have no idea if it's going to work. And obviously, I have to wait for the police to decide what they're doing with it. Even if it's not this specific track, that's what I want to do."

"Well, when you have your new grand opening, we'll be there to support you," Maggie reached across the table and offered him her hand.

"I truly appreciate the support. And I have to say it's kind of a relief to find people who understand what it's like to walk through life with this immense talent that some people take for granted. Or treat you like you're disposable, because they think it's a weakness."

"I come from a family that doesn't believe magic is real. At least my parents don't. It drove me to leave England and move here. But there is something about this place that just lets you be free." Sage was right that this town had a way of bringing things out in people, for good or ill. "But you have a truly amazing gift. And I think you should talk to my landlord and friend Tania if you ever start to feel overwhelmed. I think your gifts are similar enough that she might be able to be a really good mentor. I know she's been an amazing one for me."

"I will definitely take her up on any help she can give me." Just then, Ryan's phone buzzed with a bevy of incoming texts. He studied the screen in silence for a moment before letting out a surprised laugh. "Apparently, Jayka had the same idea about creating a collaborative effort for the track because she wants to meet and talk it over."

"Great minds think alike and all that," Vinnie said, shoving his own phone deeper in his pocket.

Ryan caught the gesture and gave his cousin a playful shove in the ribs again. Tension vanished as we fell into a companionable silence, filled by the white noise of the other cafe patrons. Equilibrium in Brookhaven had been reclaimed once more. Looking at my friends smiling faces, I just hoped it would last.

A QUICK AUTHOR'S NOTE

I won't lie, I'm not really a horse person. I did a Girl Scout horsing riding camp in elementary school and it was not a fun experience (turns out I'm allergic to hay). But, I did think it was a pretty interesting place to set a cozy mystery. And after revealing Vinnie's magical family in High Spirits, I wanted to explore that a little more.

It was definitely a different approach, having Vinnie be working alongside Darcy and company on the outer bounds of the law since he wasn't technically investigating. But I think it helped strengthen his bond with Darcy and cement him asa true ally and friend. And we got to explore Darcy's situation (albeit in reverse) with Vinnie being the non-magical one that wasn't accepted by his magic-wielding relatives. It felt like a nice juxtaposition to what we've seen from Darcy so far, and I like to think it sets the stage later down the line for a possible paradigm shift in Darcy's own personal life.

It was also fun starting to lay some more breadcrumbs for the stories that still await Darcy nd company down the line. While there weren't any big ones set for book 8, there are some things that eagle-eyed readers should file away for book 9.

Speaking of book 8, *High Wire*, I think it is my second-most favorite book of the series. Not to spoil the fun but as soon as I decided on certain reveals earlier in the series, I knew this book was coming and it puts people in even more uncomfortable places and in unfamiliar light.

Turn the page for a glimpse at High Wire...

HIGH WIRE

It's murder under the big top!

Summer fun has come to Brookhaven once again and Darcy is ready to enjoy the warm weather and outdoor festivities. Her relationship with Maggie couldn't be any better and she finally feels like she's earned her place among Brookhaven's population. When a traveling circus comes to town, she jumps at the chance to take in the fantastical acts. Not everyone is pleased to have the travelers around.

Not all is as it seems beneath the bright lights and

high-flying stunts. There's something mystical about the way the Master of Ceremonies lures people in. And when he turns up dead, things take a turn for the weird. Chief Hayes may have found the body, but he has no recollection of why he's covered in the dead man's blood.

Before long, suspicions mount that the chief could actually be the culprit. Secrets about his mysterious shapeshifting past come to light that only serve to tighten the proverbial noose around his neck. Refusing to believe a man so hell bent on upholding law and order would stoop to murder, Darcy sets out to prove his innocence. The deeper she digs, the more suspects emerge. Finding the real culprit may prove as death-defying as the high wire acts that drew her in.

Scan the QR code to buy High Wire

ABOUT THE AUTHOR

S.E. Biglow is the pen name of *USA Today* bestselling author Sarah Biglow. She lives in Massachusetts with her husband and son. She is a licensed attorney and spends her days combatting employment discrimination as an Investigator with the Massachusetts Commission Against Discrimination.

You can find an up-to-date list of all my books here